Twined

RENEE ROCCO

ONCE UPON A TWISTED ROMANCE
RENEEROCCO.COM

TWINED

Cover and Interior Design: Renee Rocco

Developmental Editor: Cassandra Higgins

Copy Editor: ACourtofSpicyEdits

First Electronic Edition: January 2023

First Print Edition: January 2023

Printed in the United States of America

Welcome to my imagination, where the villains are the heroes. My stories may include triggers for some readers. Listing (the numerous) warnings here might be seen, to some, as spoilers.

For a list of warnings, please visit my website: https://reneerocco.com/content-warnings

For everyone who fell in love with Quinn.
This one's for you.

"Did I ever tell you I've got a thing for brunettes?"

FLYNN RIDER, TANGLED

Glycerine by Bush
Mouth by Bush
The Undertaker by Puscifer
Darkside by Neoni
Unstoppable by Sia
Saddens by Enigma
Fumbling Towards Ecstasy by Sarah McLachlan
The Mummers' Dance by Loreena McKennitt
Demons by Imagine Dragons
Bring Me to Life by Evanescence
Tainted Love by Marilyn Manson
Bodies by Drowning Pool
Falling Away From Me by Korn

Listen to the full playlist
https://spoti.fi/3un4FB0

Rygard
Warton Castle
Loslow
Newkirk Castle
Aberdeen
Barrows
Kenilworth Village
Cullbury
Bryer Castle
Ainsley Castle
Lansing Village
Penbury Castle
Oakley Village
Leeds Village
Bradbury
Rapunzel's Tower
Leighton Falls
Haversvlle Village
Blythe Forest
Dyhurst Castle
Felkirk Village
Lennox Sea
Harford Castle
N
W
E
S

Chapter One

JOHN

"A single word and this torment ends."

Sybil swipes ropes of dirty hair from her face, where wrinkles have etched their way across her ashen flesh during the months she's rotted away inside my dungeon. I've taken pleasure in watching her youth and beauty fade. Oh, how I've enjoyed witnessing Rapunzel's magic drain from this witch's body, leaving her a brittle, old woman. One whose persistence and devotion, although admirable, are foolish. It's also unfortunate, given how her perseverance has worn my patience down to a raw nerve. I've wasted too much time already indulging in her misguided loyalty to Rapunzel.

It ends today. In this cell, rank with her stink because I've denied the witch even the most basic of humane necessities.

I have not even provided her with clean water.

This is the punishment for choosing the wrong side in my kingdom.

Her food rivals the slop tossed in the swine pens. Urine overflows to puddle around her chamber pot. Lice and fleas have made a home on her abused, frail body. The only comfort afforded her is a straw mattress with a single, threadbare linen blanket soiled with the body fluids of the man I had slaughtered days before this cell became her tomb.

And yet, Sybil's irritating spirit rages around her like a protective cloak. I've grown exasperated with her fortitude. The need to bring this witch to heel has become an obsession. One that burns so hot, it's almost as fervent as my need to find Rapunzel.

"Inadequate." Her croaked reply is pushed past cracked lips. Her fetid breath fills the space between us.

I tilt my head, my ear toward her, waiting to hear more. When she remains stubbornly silent, I snarl, "Explain."

"Greater men have failed to break me." Sybil straightens her spine. The chain attached to the manacle around her throat rattles with the movement. "You. Are. Inadequate." Her eyes spark with fury, and I know if she had access to her herbs and talismans, she'd cast a spell to drop me dead where I stand. Confirming this, she spits, "To the devil with you."

"I'll meet him in due time. But you'll see him first," I bite out, refusing to rise to her bait. Instead, I gesture at her kneeling at my feet and collared to the wall like a feral dog. Her reach is limited in the already tight cell, and I remain out of her grasp. The fat ruby on my finger catches in the dim light of the torch flickering from the single wall sconce beyond the rusted bars. I hold out my hand to admire the jewel. "Why do you insist on fighting me?"

Sybil shakes her head, the thick cuff around her neck tight enough to dig a bloody trench into her flesh. Her rattling breath echoes throughout the dank and claustrophobic prison. "To explain devotion and honor to you would be like explaining the heavens to an insect."

Her remark warrants a slap across her bony face. A crimson slash follows the path of my ring. Repulsed, I clean away the filth of her from my skin with a slide of my palm along my blue silk tunic. "You are many things, Sybil of Aberdeen, but I never expected foolish to be among them." I flex my fingers, revolted that I still detect her grime on my skin. When I focus back on her, I note how she's desperately fighting to hide her shivering under the weight of the dungeon's oppressive chill. "Tell me where you put my daughter and I'll provide you with clothing and a warm meal."

This irritating exchange has gone on far too long. Three months too long. The repetition of her enduring the techniques of my best torturer is getting tiresome. Also, time is running out.

Damn her.

The stubborn witch, with her gray hair hanging over her face in matted ropes, sags, lowers her head and heaves out a heavy sigh. Then she pitches forward until her palms slap against the dirty stone floor. Her body is racked with violent tremors, and I smile, satisfied.

Perhaps today *is* the day that moves me one step closer to reuniting with Rapunzel.

"I know the evil that festers within you, John." Sybil's rasp barely breaks the quiet.

I charge toward her but skid to a halt. Her foulness permeates through the fabric of my divinely granted royalty. "You know nothing!"

"Why, in all the time you've had me here, have you not demanded I weave a spell to—?"

A second slap silences her. After licking blood from the corner of her mouth, she peers at me from between that tangled hair. The dark gray of her abysmal eyes makes a slight shift to an unholy shade of obsidian, piercing through my flesh and bone. Straight to my secrets. I should rip those all-seeing orbs from their sockets and shove them down her throat to watch her choke on them.

"Do you think me a simpleton, witch?" Frustration has me stamping my foot, and it takes effort to calm my temper. "I trusted you and it killed my wife. Now, your days of spell-casting are over and once I have Rapunzel, I will become an unstoppable force. As for you," I stab a finger at her. "You'll rot down here in this dungeon until you're nothing more than dust."

"Oh, I'll be dust soon enough." She shifts, her bones creaking. Pride, I'm sure, provides her with a bit of strength. "I gave Rapunzel life from the dying Queen's last breath. I raised your daughter, King John of Rygard, and I raised her well." Her disdain drips with my title floating in the air. "There is nothing of you in that woman. Nothing at all. She will sooner burn herself alive than give up one hair to the monster you have become."

"We shall see, won't we?" I lock my hands behind my back. Tuck my lips under my teeth and nod my head, contemplating her fervent statement. Then I blink a time or two and soften my expression, my grin falsely benevolent. "Until now, I've been charitable toward you." I unlock my hands and crouch low until we're at eye level. "But I've grown weary of your insolence. Your agony will be legendary."

"Do your worst, John." Sybil spits at my feet. "But be forewarned, I'll protect your daughter until my dying breath."

"Let's test your bravery when I have you on the rack." I straighten to my full height, fury at her audacity slithering through my veins. "I've heard warriors twice your size beg for mercy as I tied the ropes around their wrists and ankles. And even more who were willing to slaughter their own children as the ropes pulled apart their joints."

"You are an abomination." Her hiss worms its way deep inside my ear, ricocheting inside my skull. I bat at the side of my head as if to dislodge the sound, then growl at Sybil's feeble sorcery trick. "How dare you *ever* call yourself Rapunzel's father. You don't deserve that title, much less that of King."

The venom in her barb might strike me if I were anything less than a king, but God himself appointed me. And she... This filthy, half-mad creature at my feet... She is beneath me. She is nothing. A scab. "And you are living on borrowed time, mongrel. As such, you have no voice." I whip around to face the open metal door of Sybil's cell, where the jailer awaits my order. "Come, Giles. Do you have your knife?" Then I turn back to Sybil, ignoring the defiant gleam in her disturbing eyes. "Let's make this interesting, shall we?"

Giles, a burly man missing one eye, slides his blade from its sheath at his left hip as he enters the cell. He scratches his round gut with his free hand, then points at Sybil. "Aye, Your Majesty." The revolting man holds the dagger up for me to inspect. "I am always your humble servant."

As well he should be. I am, after all, his fucking king.

"Silence this witch." Lest she speak of what she sees when she peers past my flesh.

May she never whisper a word of what festers inside me.

Severing Sybil's tongue will also ensure she'll never cast another spell. As it should be. When I first found her and placed her in the dungeon, I offered to provide her with all the supplies she would need to weave her magic. The obstinate woman refused to use her power for my benefit. She can't use her power against me without her tongue.

As the brute of a man advances on her, the witch scrambles across the floor, kicking up dust around her withered form as she futilely tries to scurry from him. The chain jerks her to a violent halt when it reaches its limit and I snicker at her choked gasp when she lands in a pathetic heap of flailing, skeletal limbs.

She holds up her hands, dirt caked into the chafed skin. "Wait."

"Last words?" My question stops Giles.

Has the threat of her losing her craft finally cracked her courage?

"I'll tell you of the tower." Sybil draws her legs under her and wraps her arms around her shivering body and stares back at me with wild eyes.

I stay Giles with the slightest twitch of my fingers. "What tower?"

"Oh, it's a fine tower." Sybil glances up at the ceiling as if gazing at the sky. "You should see it. I built Rapunzel a majestic haven of gray stone. One so tall, its single spire scrapes the clouds." She stretches her skeletal arms up high before dropping them back down. Her palms slap against the filthy floor.

I want to shake the answer free from her frail body. But I keep my distance, fearing the vermin crawling on her will jump on me. "Is that where I will find Rapunzel? Tell, me witch!"

"Is. Was. Will be." The witch cackles as if laughing at a jest only she knows. Then she grows serious. "Listen, and I shall tell you a story, John. Once upon a time, a witch cursed a forest. Blithe in name only, this forest was doomed not just to keep intruders out but also to keep one extraordinary little girl hidden within. This girl lived her life chained inside a tower. But I'll tell you a secret, King of Rygard. The chain wasn't to keep her from leaving. It was to keep her from suffering the guilt of *staying*. But one day, Fate spoke to the witch. It came by an opportunity she spied skulking among the ancient trees that line the bank of the Merrie River. Fate whispered to the witch of destiny. Of endings and beginnings. Of freedoms and captivity. But most of all, it spoke of love, loss, and freedom." She shrugs her slight shoulders. "Maybe Rapunzel is there, still tethered to her tower." She drags a ragged nail along the length of the chain securing her to the cell. "Or perhaps she's flown far away on the wings of a bird. Fly away, Rapunzel. Fly far, far away—"

"Enough!" My demand cuts off Sybil's manic rambling. "Take it. Take her fucking tongue."

Giles charges forward and grabs Sybil's face in his meaty grip, but the witch isn't looking at him. Her defiant gaze remains fixed on me. She doesn't fight him. She opens her mouth wide. Willingly sticks out her tongue. And right before the jailor makes the messy hack, the mad bitch winks at me. *Winks*. Is this her way of warning me the damage has already been done the day I begged her to save Anne's life? That's the day the magic passed through my dying wife's pregnant body and entered my unborn daughter.

The day Sybil cursed us all.

I should have torn the kingdom apart to find Rapunzel all those years ago. But I was a man distraught over the loss of his family. I believed Sybil's lies when she told me the child died along with my wife. Secrets, however, have a way of revealing themselves. They always do, and I should have searched for Rapunzel when I discovered she survived her birth.

But I thought I had time.

Time, however, has a way of running out.

A now familiar ache pierces my back, reminding me that this is my reward for showing my child mercy. After I find her—and I *will* find her—the magic she possesses will make me a living god, and Rygard—no, the *world*—will cower at my feet.

Rapunzel owes me for saving her life when I brought in Sybil to cast that cursed spell.

I will not tolerate an ungrateful daughter.

Especially one who is to blame for killing the only person I've ever loved.

"Rapunzel fights like she fucks, aggressive and fearless," I remark, watching her glide across the training ground with hard-earned skill.

Although Quinn has her on the defensive, it doesn't last long. A few parries followed by a handful of well-timed attacks gains her the upper hand. But while Quinn, having surrendered his soul for superhuman strength, can quickly overtake her, he's holding back to keep the mock battle honest.

With a jerk of my chin, I gesture to the lists. "He has only himself to blame for his sorry predicament."

"But look at him. Quinn is a blissful man," Dax remarks.

An exaggeration, but I concede our soulless friend seems happy. Which is miraculous, given that I'd begun to wonder if he even remembered how to smile. Now, here he is, grinning like a fool while Rapunzel slices him to shreds.

Determination and ruthless physical drive improved her swordsmanship from nonexistent to adequate in such a short time. She has no choice but to push herself almost to the breaking point. Still, I don't like her plan. None of us do. But I can't sway her. Truth be told, Rapunzel is right.

She alone can get inside Newkirk Castle.

But God forbid she goes in defenseless.

Shallow lacerations bleed from Quinn's bare chest, the blood lost among the black, vine-like markings left behind after he made his deal with the demon. The gash across his right cheek looks deep, and when he gives a curt shake of his head, sweat sprays like raindrops from his shaggy, dark hair.

Quinn lands a strike that opens a nasty gash across Rapunzel's left biceps. Dax and I know better than to rush to her defense.

She would try to separate our heads from our shoulders if we dared to interfere.

It would also defeat the purpose of her learning how to defend herself.

Thankfully, she's doing fine on her own.

Momentum drives her sword arm sweeping in a wide arc. She sucks in a sharp breath at the damage and glances at the fat line of blood that seeps from the wound. Then she lowers her head and tucks her chin, taking Quinn's measure through the fringe of her thick lashes.

Her eyes spark with green fire as she shakes her head, sending her long golden braid swaying behind her. "That wasn't nice, Quinn Redgrave."

Her audacity is stunning.

A work of art.

Quinn smirks. "You don't like me nice."

"True."

The magic infused in the golden strands of her knee-length hair closes the wound almost instantly. Quinn's take longer, but only by a little. Together, however, they make for a nearly indestructible pair. The only evidence of Rapunzel's injury is the torn and blood-stained sleeve of her white shirt.

Not too long ago—three months, four days, to be exact—Rapunzel considered her gift a curse. Shame still claws at me when I think of how I'm one of the reasons she hated her healing magic. That guilt is a crushing weight on my shoulders. It's a constant reminder that I blamed her for King John's sins.

The bastard murdered my parents. He's destroying Rygard in his manic hunt to find Rapunzel. John even captured Sybil—the witch who kidnapped Rapunzel and cursed an entire forest to keep her hidden.

Now John has the witch locked up tight in Newkirk. Our spies told us she cast him only a single spell—the poison that nearly killed Quinn. Who knows what more she'll do for him or what secrets she'll spill after enough time and torture?

Transfixed, Dax and I watch Rapunzel. She took to the sword as if she were born to wield one. Albeit hers is custom crafted for her tiny hands. But my *God*. She swings the weapon with astounding grace and purpose.

She advances when she sees an opening, putting Quinn on the defensive. The usually ill-tempered former knight widens his grin. The expression lifts the scar that cuts down his left cheek, giving him a menacing edge that doesn't intimidate Rapunzel.

"And *nice* is Dax's weakness, Princess," Quinn snarls at her. "Not mine."

While that's true, I know Quinn finds it as appalling as we do to train Rapunzel since none of us willingly want to harm a hair on her pretty head. Especially knowing the cost of damaging those enchanted waves. It's more challenging for him, given the tight rein he must keep on his strength.

"Tell me, what's your weakness, Quinn Redgrave?"

He gives her a barely perceptible shake of the head. "I don't have one. Now fucking hurt me, Princess, *if you can*."

Lie.

Everyone has a vulnerability, even Quinn.

But his taunt works because Rapunzel's upper lip curls into a snarl as she charges, unhindered by skirts. For practicality's sake, she wears breeches while training. Quinn could swat her away as easily as he would a fly, but he allows her an opening to see if she'll take it. Damn it all if she does. The woman is incredible as she performs a feints blow, then follows it with a kick to Quinn's stomach. The perfectly executed move has him giving her a curt nod of approval. Rather than retreat when Quinn counterattacks, she parries. Spins. Slashes. Her blade opens a deep gash across his abdomen.

"Oh, look." Panting, Rapunzel adjusts her hold on the weapon's hilt, keeping the sword at the ready. "It bleeds."

"Well played." Quinn's smooth voice reverberates across the lists. But like us, he knows it will take more than a few sword lessons to defeat the king. It's why we bring her out to the lists each day, pushing Rapunzel past her limit. Why we practice this dance of attack and defense.

A dance of kill or be killed.

"Remind me what I told you about fairness in battle." The sharpness of Quinn's tone is tantamount to that of his sword.

"There isn't any."

"Exactly," he growls.

Dax and I cringe at the exact moment Quinn sweeps Rapunzel's legs out from under her. She lands on her back with a solid thud. Although dazed, she maintains her grip on her weapon. Quinn mounts her and presses his knee on her wrist. The pressure renders her right arm—her sword arm—useless.

"Yield."

"I don't yield," she grits out between clenched teeth. "Ever."

"You are defeated, Princess." Quinn's blood drips onto her clothes—and fuck it all if she's not a stunning temptation lying beneath him in those breeches. The garment molds to the gentle curve of her hips as she bucks them in a valiant but vain attempt to dislodge him. She kicks out, her legs unhindered by a cumbersome gown and chemise. "Yield to me."

Dax elbows me in the ribs. "A week of emptying our chamber pots says she surrenders."

"Our girl?" Never. "The sun will sooner drop from the sky before Rapunzel surrenders."

"He's persuasive," Dax drawls.

"True, he's a bully, but you are a fool if you underestimate her."

Rapunzel proves she learned to fight unfairly when, with her free hand, she punches Quinn in the groin. His howl drowns out our laughter. He reels backward and lands on his ass, allowing Rapunzel to pop up and plant her dainty booted foot on his throat. A throat that three months ago was sliced wide by one of John's soldiers with a blade tainted with Sybil's poison. If Rapunzel hadn't used a lock of her hair to save his life, Quinn would have died right where we're standing.

She levels the blade at his face, the point inches from his eye. "Yield to me."

Snorting out a laugh because Dax will be cleaning our piss and shit for a sennight, I clap him on the back. "I wouldn't want to be you, my friend."

"To hell with that." Dax cups his hands around his mouth and yells, "Don't tell me you're going to yield to a woman more than half your size." With a voice laced with humor, he adds, "By God's teeth, Quinn, I do believe she'll dig out your eye."

"Fuck it." Quinn's restricted growl makes us laugh harder. "I'll grow another."

"So stubborn," Rapunzel *tsks*. She brings the blade closer. "But I'm stubborn as well. Yield."

"Take the fucking eye."

We know why Quinn is pushing her. Because one day in the extremely near future, Rapunzel will be alone in John's court. She may be his daughter and Rygard's rightful heir, but to him, she's nothing more than a vessel. A means to achieve more power. He wants her magic, and if she doesn't give it to him willingly, John will try to take it by force. We must prepare her to do more than survive—but also to survive the king.

Survive him long enough for us to kill him…even if that preparation includes her destroying Quinn's eye during this sparring session.

Rapunzel wavers. The movement is slight, but it's the opening Quinn needs. In one fluid motion, he overtakes her. Her sword flies from her hand to land uselessly out of reach. He slams her on her back again and, this time forces her legs apart and fits himself in the space he created. Tosses his weapon aside —to prove to her none is needed. Effortlessly tames her flailing arms by trapping them in one hand and slapping them above her head. The press of his hips keeps her from wriggling out from under him. Propped up on one arm, he brings his face so close to hers that their lips brush.

"Like this, you're mine." His voice is angry, hissed out against her mouth. "If I wanted, I could cut every strand of hair from your head and watch you die on the ground. Or…" He leans away and burns her with his hungry gaze. "I could rape you until you *wish* you were dead." Then he brings his lips to her ear but says loud enough for us to hear, "Next time you fell your opponent, you fucking finish him. Do you understand me, Rapunzel?"

"I understand." Her whisper barely reaches Dax and me, and although I want to pull Quinn off her, I also understand this lesson.

And approve.

Rapunzel needs to be more scared of suffering the consequences of defeat than following through with harming a person —even if it's someone she cares about.

"Good." Quinn releases her wrists and pushes himself to his feet. He extends a hand to her in peace. Rapunzel accepts, and only after she's steady on her feet does he feather his lips over her knuckles. "You did well today. I'm proud of you."

She averts her gaze. "In the end, I showed weakness."

Quinn places a finger under her chin, forcing her to look

back at him. "If taking a life was easy, the world would be a graveyard." He claims her mouth in a rough kiss that leaves her more dazed than when he knocked her to the ground. "There's no shame in defeat if you come away with a lesson learned. So, tell me, what lesson did you learn today?"

"Next time, take the eye."

He retrieves her sword and presents it to her, hilt first. "Never trust your enemy, and never claim victory until your opponent is dead."

Rapunzel accepts her weapon dismally. "I'm sorry I hurt you."

Quinn stabs a finger in her face. "And don't *ever* fucking apologize for defending yourself."

Duly chastised, she gives him a solemn nod. "Never again." She slides her weapon into the sheath belted around her trim waist. Then she extends her hand for him to shake. "Peace?"

He also sheaths his sword but ignores her hand and drapes a tattooed arm around her shoulders. The markings look as if he dipped his hands in black ink, and it dripped up his forearms. "You are the only thing in this miserable world that gives me joy, Princess." He tugs her in closer against his side and kisses the side of her head. "I starve. Let's bother Bryce and see what that ornery prick is roasting in the kitchen." They stroll toward the keep, with Quinn saying to Dax and me from over his shoulder, "You wenches coming with us, or are you going to stand there gossiping all morning?"

"I'm going to kill him one of these days."

At Dax's empty promise, Quinn grunts out a laugh. "I'm not so hungry that we can't have a go right now."

Dax kicks the back of Quinn's knee, causing our soulless friend to wobble. "It's been a while since I beat the shit out of you."

Having been with us long enough, Rapunzel leaps out of harm's way.

Quinn palms his sword. "A while? Try never, you bastard."

"Damned right, I'm a bastard." Dax Stafford's father, Sir Simon Baines, never claimed him. The two men met once, which apparently was enough for both of them. "And I believe you reminded Rapunzel that all is fair in battle. Or am I mistaken?"

"Come to me, Rapunzel." I hold out my hand. "This is going to get ugly."

"Anything with Quinn in it is ugly," Dax quips.

"Ugly. Bloody. Same difference." Quinn, walking backward toward the lists, twirls his broadsword.

Rapunzel runs to me and wraps her arms around my waist, and it's the most natural thing for me to kiss the side of her head. Fuck. There was a time when I feared I'd never touch this woman. Back when she was locked in that goddamn tower, and I was stuck on the outside desperately trying to convince her to come away with me. Now she's mine. *Ours*. I planned to share her with Quinn and Dax as a means of degradation. As an act of revenge after I learned her hair had the power to heal the sick and the injured. I hated her for doing nothing when she could have saved my father from the poison John used to kill him.

Instead, Rapunzel rejoiced in her freedom. She reveled in our touch after a lifetime of loneliness. Now, when the four of us are together, we are at our strongest.

We're aware our relationship breaks every societal rule, and if the nine other renegades who live within Dyhurst Castle's walls oppose our arrangement, they keep their opinion private. Although more often than not we're discreet with open displays of passion, we don't hide our affection for Rapunzel.

And what an eclectic clan we have here. Each man here is a former member of the royal military. Emma Heathe of Weston, a noble who witnessed her family struck down by John, was the lone woman until Rapunzel made our family complete.

Hatred for the king brought us together.

Kinship keeps us together and thriving.

May Quinn and Dax remember this as steel clashes on the lists.

The noise draws the attention of Arthur, as always he is busy tending the garden. Usually, Rapunzel and Emma toil in the dirt with him, but not these last few weeks. Not when training Rapunzel takes precedence over all else. The commotion even brings out some other men to watch the melee.

Emma, though, barges through the crowd of four massive men. Wiping her hands on the apron tied around her waist, she marches up to us. Rapunzel and I stand on the edge of lists watching as Dax and Quinn beat on each other. They've already drawn blood, and while Quinn's ass has taken the brunt of Dax's sword, something tells me Dax sliced him there purposely.

Emma swipes stray chestnut strands of hair away from her eyes. "One day, Quinn is going to kill that man."

"It's all in good fun." Tristan, arms crossed over his broad chest, spits on the ground. He mutters something to Ian that has the fair-haired truant royal soldier chuckling.

Also, it makes for great entertainment.

"Quinn would never hurt Dax," Rapunzel announces. She's still sweaty from her fight. When Quinn whips around and uses the hilt of his sword to strike Dax hard between the shoulder blades, she adds, "Although it does seem like he's having a bit *too* much fun."

Dax, who was trained by the best, puts up a damn decent fight but loses gained ground when Quinn lunges. Quinn follows through with a flurry of offensive moves that drives Dax backward. Cursing, Dax counters with rapid strikes that tear at Quinn's arms and chest, shredding him.

Rather than put Dax back on the defensive, Quinn jumps away, wipes sweat from his brow and cringes when he glances at the damage to his body. "I yield."

"Aye. Same," Dax agrees, heaving. He inspects a rather nasty gash on his forearm before sheathing his sword. "Unlike you and our lady, I don't have the power to heal. Emma, sweetling, would you be so kind as to get your needle and thread? I require your superior sewing skills."

"Perhaps if I use my superior sewing skills to stitch his mouth closed, he wouldn't have this issue," she mumbles. Then louder, "How can I deny you when you ask so nicely?" She gestures at Dax. "That one knows you get more flies with honey than vinegar. Now, you mind your men while I fetch my kit."

"I'll try, but they tend to misbehave," Rapunzel calls after her.

Rapunzel speaks no lie. We do misbehave, but she doesn't seem to mind…especially not when she's the recipient of our depraved behavior. But what Emma fails to realize is that her deceptively gentle friend is as wicked as we are.

Once Emma is far enough away and the men have dispersed, it's just the four of us on the lists. Rapunzel rushes to Quinn to inspect his bleeding body.

Tsking, she traces her elegant fingers along each healing wound. "Why do you allow them to hurt you?"

His dark eyes spark with malicious delight. "You, of all people, know I enjoy the pain."

Rapunzel's cheeks flush, and I can practically hear her thoughts. Quinn certainly does like his pleasure laced with a healthy dose of torture. Makes me wonder if he always had this inclination or if it came after he bartered away his soul. She slides her hands down his arms, then intertwines her fingers with his. "If I can't be needlessly reckless with my body, neither can you."

"It's not at all the same," he growls.

I come up behind her and rest my hands on the curve of her hips. She exhales on a slow breath when I press my lips to her racing pulse below her ear. "I speak for us all, Your Highness, when I offer a humble apology for injuring poor, defenseless Quinn."

"Cease goading him," she scolds me. Then, "And spare me

your false humility. I know you too well, Wren Kincaid. There isn't a humble bone in your arrogant body."

"They're safe from my wrath. For now." Quinn drags his tongue along her lower lip. "I'd much rather spend the rest of the afternoon finding creative ways to atone for worrying you."

Our usual discretion be damned. The courtyard is deserted, and Rapunzel is too delectable of a temptation to resist.

"I'd love to see you try." Rapunzel molds her back to my chest, arching her spine just enough to cause her breasts to strain against the coarse material of her shirt. Quinn seizes the moment and rubs the pad of his thumb over her erect nipple. She rests her head against my shoulder. "You scoundrels are too crafty for your own good."

"We are indeed." Dax comes up beside her, the cut bleeding down his hand. He grips her chin with his wet fingers and forces her to turn toward him, an arrogant, crooked grin tugging at his mouth. "And tonight, when my cock hits the back of your throat, you'll show us how devious you are as well, Little Captive."

She snakes an arm around Dax's waist to tug him closer. "Don't I always?"

Watching Dax tease her, mouth open in a fevered kiss, sends a rush of blood straight to my cock. Their tongues glide as he moves his other hand between her legs. Her whimper mingles with Quinn's guttural growl. And when I trace my fingers up along her ribcage, she gasps into Dax's mouth and presses into my touch. Quinn torments the hard peaks of her breasts, barely hidden by her flowing shirt, while I stroke her sides. I run my hands up her spine then trail a single finger down until I reach her ass, where I travel farther still, low enough to hear her gasp into Dax's kiss.

"I can smell your desire, Princess." Quinn rasps that in her ear. "Tonight, I intend to taste it."

Unfortunately, we're forced to break apart when Emma throws open the door of the keep. Sewing kit in hand, she calls for Dax. Rapunzel wipes his blood from her chin with a trembling hand, then drags in a ragged breath and backs away. She adjusts her shirt. Grabs her long, golden braid and pulls it over her shoulder to smooth a hand over the twisted waves. All the while, a sly little grin curls her lips. And once we join Emma in the hall, the commanding woman sits Dax in front of the hearth, she cleans the wound before sewing his injury closed.

Throughout the ordeal, Rapunzel refuses to leave Dax's side while Quinn and I see what monstrosity is brewing in the kitchen. One drawback of training Rapunzel to fight is that she no longer has time to help with the meals. We're back to suffering Bryce's sad offerings. But it's a pittance we're willing to pay to ensure she'll be at least somewhat prepared when she faces her father.

Once he's dead and Rapunzel takes her rightful place on Rygard's throne, she'll return peace to this kingdom. That's the goal we're working toward. What goes unsaid between us is that we're living on borrowed time with her. Every moment spent with her is precious because this—*this* is the quiet before the storm.

Chapter Three

DAX

This storm is relentless.

Rain has battered our rugged peninsula for the better part of last night and throughout the morning. With the courtyard sodden and Emma and Bryce busy in the kitchen, Rapunzel was of a mind to join them.

Not on my watch.

I have other plans for our lovely, golden-haired lady.

Didn't take much to convince Rapunzel I needed her elsewhere.

My bed was lonely without her—and God has yet to create a prettier sight than this woman lying naked with those thick waves spread out around her.

Although confident by nature, I find myself ten thumbs and two left feet when it's the two of us. Everything about this woman robs me of the arrogance gained from surviving countless battles and many dalliances with nameless and faceless women. From the sparkle of mischief in her brilliant green eyes, right down to the adorable toes of her tiny feet, her lithe body is made to worship. And with Quinn and Wren suffering the elements while tending to the horses in the stables, she and I have the morning to ourselves.

Rarely are we alone, and when she reaches her arms out to me, beckoning me, I'm suddenly a nervous boy fumbling with the laces of my breeches. I kick off my boots before dragging my pants down my legs. Then I push Emma's mending skills to its limit by practically ripping off my shirt.

Her tender expression warms me more than the fire blazing in the hearth. "Clothing is a crime on you, Dax Stafford."

"Odd." I take her hand and twine my fingers around hers after I climb on the bed. "Here I am thinking the same of you, Little Captive."

She may no longer be Wren's hostage, but I haven't stopped calling her by the name I gave her after he took her from the tower. "Good thing we seldom wear them when we're alone."

"True." I haul her to her knees, bringing her face inches from mine. Her body is close enough that her wonderfully hard nipples press against my solid chest. Then I swing her arm around. Pin her wrist to the small of her back, locking her in place right where I want her. "I'm still astounded how you survived twenty-four years in the awful place by yourself."

This woman is unbridled passion. I can't fathom how she didn't perish from loneliness long before Wren dragged her from that miserable tower deep within Blithe Forest.

The brush of her lips is a bolt of lightning straight to the tip of my painfully hard cock. "How could I miss what I never experienced?" She puts her lips to my ear, her melodic voice as soothing as it is seductive. "But I yearned, Dax." The audacious woman looks me right in the eyes as she reaches between our bodies to stroke my shaft. "God, how I yearned. Every night I'd lie in bed staring into the dark and imagining all the ways I wanted to be touched."

That deft hand certainly knows how to touch *me*. She

squeezes the fat tip of my cock. Precum wets her palm to ease her slide down to the base. "You imagined it was Wren."

Her coy grin nails me in the heart even as she continues to work me with her hand. I hiss when her deft fingers slide over the sensitive spot on the underside of my cock's head. "I knew no one else." She nips my bottom lip. Licks it. Kisses me good and hard. "I need you, Dax. Not Wren or Quinn. *You*." She stops stroking me to take my hand and place it between her legs. "Please, help keep the memories of those lonely years at bay."

"Rapunzel." Her name is an ecstasy and an agony. I release her wrist to dig my hand into her hair, letting the silken strands cascade through my fingers. The bastard that I am, I have no business rising above my station even to breathe the same air as this woman. But here I am, holding Rygard's greatest treasure in my hands. "All of me belongs to all of you."

"I've always belonged to you before I even knew you. To the three of you." Her sex is wet and warm against my palm. I slide a finger up her seam to her clit. She presses her lips to mine. "That's nice."

"Nice?" I *tsk*. Then I lick the intoxicating taste of her from my finger before pressing it back against her clit. I circle the swollen nub, pulling a tantalizing moan from her. "Seems I shall have to do better, won't I?"

"Foolish man. You know your talents. I'm merely trying to keep your ego in check."

"Cheeky wench." I give Rapunzel's pussy a playful tap. "Now, be a good girl. Let me have my wicked way with you."

Rapunzel does as she's told without argument. Publicly, she is Rygard's rightful heir. Alone with us, she surrenders to our command. She lies back on the bed with the glow of the firelight accenting the delicate hills and valleys of her soft curves. She opens her legs and stares at me with hooded eyes. There is a challenge in those mesmerizing depths. "How wicked?"

I trace a finger along her jawline. Down her throat. Across

her collarbone. Finally, I tease the taut peaks of her pretty breasts. "How wicked do you want me, Little Captive?" She arches her back when I squeeze and tug at her rosy nipples. Then I move farther down, and when I reach her soft, brunette curls at the juncture of her thighs, I dip two fingers inside her. "Is this wicked enough?"

She shakes her head. "Not nearly wicked enough."

I add a third finger, stretching her, and stroke her slow and deep. "How about this?"

Again, she shakes her head. "Do better."

"We made you greedy."

"Aye, you did." She lifts her hips and releases a long, breathy sigh as I work her cunt in a gentle torment to build her pleasure. I hook my fingers and rub the spot inside her that always elicits the sexiest moans. And between those delightful groans, she demands, "I want to watch you stroke yourself."

Never let it be said that Dax Stafford doesn't do all he can to please his woman. I'd give her anything she asks, everything she needs—including my heart. Because everything about Rapunzel is gentle and kind and makes me strive to be a better man. I never imagined much for myself that didn't involve dying on a battlefield until she stepped out of Blythe Forest, and I suddenly wanted more. Craved a lifetime spent living in the glow of her light.

My hand moves almost of its own volition. Rapunzel's eyes light with hunger as I skate my hand over my cock. Her gaze is a particular torment. I squeeze the head, then slide to the base. With my other hand, I pump into her cunt, her whispered moans stringing together to form a beautiful song that fills the room.

Her muscles tighten around my fingers as her first climax hits. The flood of her desire soaks me. It takes every bit of discipline from the years spent as a knight not to sink my cock into her right now. Which, of course, is a fine idea—but there's no need to rush. Not when this treasure is mine to savor at my leisure.

Only once the tension in her body eases, and I'm positive she's ridden out her orgasm do I pull my hands from our bodies and grab her ankles. Rapunzel gives an adorable little gasp as I drag her to the foot of the bed.

"It's been one whole day since I last had my tongue in your cunt." I drop to my knees and settle between her thighs. "Now that, Rapunzel, is a travesty we must rectify immediately."

Propped up on her elbows, she rewards me with her throaty laughter. "Truly it is, given your talent with your mouth."

"You mean other than annoying Quinn with my cutting wit?"

Her gaze flicks to the wound on my arm. "Keep taunting him, and he's going to kill you."

"Doubtful, but if it happens, I will die a satisfied man having had my face between your thighs." I give her a wink and a gentle shove on her shoulder that buckles her elbows. "Now, be a dear and lie back so I can pleasure you proper."

"Forsooth, this is the only thing "proper" about you." Rapunzel surrenders in a flop on her back, arms at her sides and fingers digging into the yellow linen blanket. The bedding was Wren's idea to brighten their otherwise dark chamber. Same with the cheerful tapestries that now decorate the stone walls. Sadly, nothing can take away from Dyhurst's bleakness. The castle's disrepair is why we chose this desolate location. It keeps John's watchful eye from finding us.

It affords us mornings such as these when I can dip my head between Rapunzel's lovely thighs and lick the slick seam of her sex to savor her sweetness.

There's no denying I've come a long way from trawling Lansing's streets as a grubby little bastard thief. Then, as a knight in the royal army. Now here I am, relishing the affection of Rygard's princess—its future queen—if all goes as we hope.

But that battle seems far off. All that matters on this stormy morning is Rapunzel.

I tease her clit, my name a guttural groan that rolls off her tongue. The devious bastard I am, I torture her a bit more. "Tell me, Little Captive, what feels better? When I do this?" I flick the tip of my tongue over her swollen clit. "Or this?" I lave her entire cunt—as if I haven't memorized exactly how our lady enjoys being licked.

I imagined no version of myself, a grubby thief or royal knight would be satisfied with one woman. Much less share one with two men. But Rapunzel is special. From the moment I touched her, everything seemed to fall into place. Like pieces of a puzzle.

"Both. I love when you do both," Rapunzel pants. "Oh, my God, Dax." She bucks, grinding her mound against my mouth. Demands the friction I'm denying her. Stabs her hands in my hair. Twists. Pulls. "More of everything. More of you. *Please*."

So wonderfully greedy. Rapunzel's beautiful abandon feeds my depraved desire. I worship her whole pussy, licking and sucking and nipping just hard enough to elicit lovely little gasps from her. My cock is so hard it hurts. I give it a few pumps to ease the building pressure as my other hand coaxes another orgasm from Rapunzel. And God's teeth, she ethereal with her glorious hair a golden halo framing her.

But we have two problems.

One, Rapunzel has strong legs from her battle training, and when her muscles tighten, she damn near crushes my skull as she rides out her climax. And two, I'm dangerously close to spilling into my hand like an eager boy with his first woman.

I'm no physician, but I'm reasonably positive I can't survive without my head. But I can't think of a better way to meet my God if I am to die.

Steadfast in my mission to meet the challenge of lasting long enough to make Rapunzel see God for the third time, I rise to my feet with determination. Wiping my mouth with the back of my hand, I give her a devious grin. "You made a mess all over my face."

She sits up and damn me if she doesn't match my lazy grin. "You *made* me make a mess all over your face."

Damn right I did.

Rapunzel leans forward, her mouth inches from my aching erection. I sink a hand in her golden hair, twining it around my fist. "Open your mouth for me."

Always obedient in the privacy of our chambers, Rapunzel does as she's told, and I press the head of my cock to her open, plump lips. I sink in deep. The flat of her tongue rubs the underside of my shaft, and fuck it's a warm, wet homecoming when I hit the back of her throat. I groan and hold myself still, swallowed by her. Committing this perfect moment to memory.

When I withdraw, she sucks in a sharp breath. The rush of air around my cock drives me mad. I slide back in, and the vibration of her moan races me toward ecstasy. But the little tease takes control, showing me no mercy because we trained her well.

"That's it." I draw my cock out and let her play. She swirls her tongue around my swollen head. Kisses her way around the tip. With her eyes locked on mine, she licks her way down the shaft, my little tease, before swallowing me down to the base. "That's my good girl. Lick it just like that."

I've studied her, and I know she enjoys skating along the edge of pain. While not my thing, I tug at her hair. She groans and sucks me harder. I pull it again—sharper this time, and at her moan, I maintain the tension in the silken strands, confident they won't snap from the strain.

I won't steal a moment of precious time from Rapunzel's life.

The magic infused in the golden waves makes it nearly indestructible—damageable only with blade or flame.

Her mouth is stretched wide to accommodate my size. I used to fear I would choke her, rip her tiny body, but she takes me so well in her pretty mouth and beautiful cunt. And while I watch her cheeks hollow at the suction of her pulls, I realize this game has gone on long enough because I'm dangerously close to coming down her throat. I pull her head away but keep my hand fisted in her hair. "Up by the head of the bed, Little Captive. It's time for you to get what you deserve. Is that what you want? Do you think you deserve my cum?"

"Deserve it?" She slides up the mattress and lays her head on the pillow. Spreads her long legs. Her pussy is wet for me. Glistening. Begging for me. She twines one hand in the rumpled blanket. Sweet God. Rapunzel cups her sex with the other and arches her back. Then she takes her fingers, drenched with her desire, and moistens her nipple. Torturing the pebbled nub. "I demand it. Fuck me, Dax."

The beautiful invitation she presents sends a shot of desire through me as I crawl up her body. Rapunzel is twenty-four years of caged passion unleashed. Primal. Unbridled fire. And when I line the head of my cock with the soaked entrance of her cunt, she lifts her hips to welcome me home.

Wound so tightly, I'm about to snap. I punch into her in one smooth, brutal plunge. Rapunzel gasps and claws at my back, her nails grazing over my fevered flesh. Her mouth parts, and I sweep my tongue past her lips in a feral kiss that robs us both of breath. I rock into her so deep my balls slap her ass.

Fuck.

I'm not lasting long.

Together, as always, we are a frenzy.

Wild and fun and free.

I pull my mouth from hers. "I love how you take my cock, Little Captive."

"You give it to me so good." She lifts her hips in time with mine, meeting each long, hard thrust. "I love the feel of you inside of me."

Frantic and raw.

Carnal.

Especially when I flip her over and pull her up on her knees. I wrap an arm around her stomach to cradle her against me, her back flush against my chest. When I slide back into her pussy, she drops her head on my shoulder and whispers the sweetest moan.

Her hand in mine, I guide us to her clit to play in the wet. Teasing her swollen cunt. Pulling desperate sounds from her as I fuck her. With my hand still covering hers, I add our fingers, stretching her wider. It adds to the friction as I pump my cock against them.

She gasps and stiffens against me. "Dax…"

"Are you my good girl, Rapunzel?"

She nods against my shoulder. "Yes."

"Good girls take what they're given." My cock glides against our fingers, against the heat of her drenched walls. "And they're grateful for the pleasure."

"Thank you. Oh, God, Dax, thank you for fucking me with your cock and our fingers."

My arm tightens around her as I rock into her again and again and again. Rasping filthy words into her ear that pull incoherent whispers from her. And when she reaches behind her head to grasp my hair, she's so goddamn pretty when she comes.

"That's it, Rapunzel." I fuck her hard and deep, using our fingers to press against my cock. "Come all over me. All over us."

Because I intend to come all over her.

Fair play, after all.

The next punch of my hips builds pressure from my spine to the head of my cock. I pull out of her and shove her forward. She lands on her hands. I toss her hair aside with one hand and jerk my cock with the other, shooting thick ropes of cum on her perfect ass.

"Fuck. Christ. Oh, Lord. Fuck," I hiss between clenched teeth.

Once the last shudder leaves me, Rapunzel attempts to crawl off the bed. I stop her. My cock wet with her pleasure, and swinging heavy between my legs, I grab a rag from the washstand. Dip it in the bowl of tepid water. Carry it back to the bed and, because I'm such a fucking gentleman, wipe my cum off her flawless skin—well, flawless save for the large handprint bruise on her ass that I suspect belongs to Quinn. Then I clean my cock before tossing the cloth on the floor. I'll pick it up later. Right at this moment, I have something better to do with my time. Like cuddling with my lovely lady.

I hold out my arms to her. Rapunzel's contentment is positively beguiling as she settles into my embrace. I love the floral soap she uses. The heady scent clings to her thick, golden hair. Hair that contains a power that can change the world.

How does someone this tiny, this delicate, possess something so powerful?

Rapunzel drapes an arm around my chest, hugging me. "I can't believe there was a time when I hated rainy days."

"In your defense, you were alone in a tower." I kiss the side of her head. "But you're not alone anymore."

"No, I'm not." There's a thick quiet between us before her soft confession cuts me to the quick. "I'm scared."

I shift so I can see her face, and there it is. Raw fear reflected in her luminous eyes. "Of what, Little Captive?"

But I know the answer.

"Failure. But also of what will happen once I make it to court. Right now, he's this abstract being. Someone more obscure than real. You've all met him. Stood in his presence. Looked him in the eye. But I'm afraid of him, Dax. Oh, God, I'm terrified of him." She lifts her head and pierces me with a pleading gaze. "Please don't tell Wren or Quinn. I don't think they will understand that even though I'm afraid I'm still prepared to do whatever is necessary to take this kingdom from him."

To murder her father.

I cup her chin. "We won't fail, Rapunzel. Do you understand me? We're going to murder that bastard, put you on the throne, and fix the goddamn mess he made of Rygard. And you don't have to be afraid of him. As you said, I stood in his presence. John may be king, but he is also just a man. You made Quinn bleed. Remember that anytime you find yourself afraid."

Her chin quivers, and her eyes sparkle with the threat of tears, but she nods, fighting for conviction. "What if I'm not a good queen?"

I smooth a hand over her hair, my smile tender and hopefully, reassuring. "Rapunzel, sweetling, if ever a woman was born to be a worthy queen, it was you."

She sacrificed her freedom because she believed she was a danger to Rygard. Every Rygardian owes her their life. We can never give her back those lost twenty-four years, but we can damn well give her our gratitude—and that starts with the three of us doing everything within our power to make sure she gets that crown.

"I pray you're right."

I twirl a lock of her hair around my finger. "I'm always right, Little Captive."

The tension leaves her body, and this time, silence falls between us when she places her head on my chest. It's a comfortable one. Eventually, though, she breaks it. "Do you hear that?"

Listening, I frown. "Not a thing."

"Exactly." She points to the ceiling. "The rain stopped. Our lazy morning is at an end."

My brows shoot up at her absurd remark. "Lazy? There was nothing lazy about what we did." I drag Rapunzel with me when I sit up. Propped against the wooden headboard, I position her on my lap. My body stirs to life when her bare ass settles over my cock. "Let's see how lazy you find the morning when you're bouncing on my cock. What say you to that?"

Leave it to Rapunzel to beat me at my game. Her grin is positively evil. "I say that's a fine idea." She lifts and notches her sex on the head of my dick. "A fine idea, indeed."

She grips my face and licks her way into my mouth. Then sucks in a sharp breath when her weight carries her down. Buried to the base, I growl as I thrust into her. But she takes control by working herself on me, as always, with primal desperation…

Because time is racing us toward a reckoning that will either be Rygard's salvation or destruction.

RAPUNZEL

"Have you considered what will happen with your…*arrangement*…once the crown is on your head?"

This is the first time Emma has commented on my relationship with Wren, Quinn, and Dax. Until now, everyone at Dyhurst has kept their own counsel. Or if they have an opinion about what we do privately, they haven't been brave enough to voice it aloud.

Not in front of us, anyway.

They wouldn't dare.

Wren and Dax would cut them down where they stood…

…if Quinn didn't rip out their throats first.

As if anyone at Dyhurst would speak a harsh word about the men who helped save them from King John's brutality. Their loyalty, forged in the wake of John's path of destruction, was sealed with blood. It is unquestionable and unbreakable.

Shielding my eyes against the afternoon sun, I pause in plucking peas from the vines that grow in the garden. Across the courtyard, Quinn and Dax are helping the men repair the western corner of the chapel's timber roof. The hammering echoes on the unseasonably warm early October morning, a welcomed relief after yesterday's downpour. The small building sustained a bit of damage during the storm. Nothing too severe, thankfully, and with almost everyone lending a hand to get it fixed, they should have Kenric back in his little stone sanctuary by nightfall.

The defrocked priest insists on sleeping in there. He claims it keeps him close to God. I, however, believe the Almighty is always with us. That we carry the Lord within our hearts. Besides, I refuse to accept God wants Kenric to sleep on a pallet on the cold floor, isolated from his family, when there's more than enough room for him in the hall. It's awful that the church forced laicization upon him for denouncing religious doctrine that harms women, and I'm sure that rejection left him with a hole in his heart.

Not all that long ago, I, too, was lost and alone. It bothers me that Kenric might find himself trapped in that same state. Albeit, his is mental. Mine was physical as well. Often, I wonder what's worse—loneliness when surrounded by people or a sense of displacement when you're exactly where you're supposed to be.

I turn away from the magnificent sight of the men of Dyhurst toiling under the autumn sun. Wren, Bryce, and Ian are missing. Bryce, as always, is busy in the kitchen preparing our daily meals. In our quest to track John's movements, Ian is away, meeting with allies from neighboring villages to find out if anyone has spotted the king's soldiers in the vicinity. And Wren, he—as always—is out hunting. If he's not pushing himself to the limit on the lists, he's in the surrounding woods, keeping everyone at Dyhurst fed.

As best he can.

Unfortunately, he's one person, and the peninsula is small. To help replenish our food stocks, Lucian and Arthur travel to Leighton Falls on market days. There is an air of tension blanketing Rygard, they tell us. As if a single moment of weakness is all it will take for John to catch us unawares. So, we stay vigilant, and we stay hidden.

The plan is for *us* to catch *John* by surprise, not the other way around.

When I glance back at Emma, she's watching me expectantly. Waiting for an answer I don't have because although we're working toward a common goal—to eliminate the king and seat me on the throne—our aim somehow still seems… outlandish. It's a goal that includes killing a king and usurping his kingdom. It's an entirely paralyzing concept on its own. But the terrifying image of my head wearing the crown has been all-consuming, pushing aside any concerns about my relationship with Wren, Dax, and Quinn.

"I haven't thought about it if you want the truth."

"Your Highness…" Her sentence trails off before she restarts because she knows I'm uncomfortable with the formality. Soon enough, I'll have to slip into the role of princess—then queen. But here, with my family, I am, and will remain… Me. "Rapunzel." She speaks my name like a punch as she tosses a handful of peas into our communal basket. "It will cause a scandal. One they will use against you."

Although I grew up isolated, locked in a tower, where I believed I would live out my days miserable and alone, I'm not ignorant. What we share isn't traditional. However, I'm confident that most 'proper' ladies wouldn't hesitate to change places with me.

Given how I've sacrificed my freedom for this kingdom, I take umbrage at Emma's observation. "Why would anyone care who I love as long as I am a good queen? Especially after John married a child bride against her will. One whom he beats. My relationships should be insignificant. What people *should* be concerned about is a life free of worry that a mad King will tax them to starvation. Or worse, burn their village to ash on a whim."

"If people did as they should, we wouldn't be in this predicament. If life were that simple, I would still have my family. Ah, Rapunzel, what a world that would be." Emma returns to plucking fat pea pods from the vine, her expression heartbreaking. "But that world does not exist. Reality is cold and cruel, and people are judgmental fools." She nods at Dax and Quinn. "Your men will defend you, yes, but as a woman, you must protect yourself against threats both seen and unseen at all times."

Being reminded of this truth is harsh but welcomed.

"I understand, and I will be cautious at court before and after we take down that bastard." Then I look her in the eye and say with conviction, "I will avenge your family, Emma. John will pay for what he's done. That monster will suffer for taking your family from you. He'll answer for the pain he's caused Rygard, and after he's gone, I'll restore peace to this kingdom. I swear this on my soul. That won't bring back your family, but I hope it will ease some of your grief."

Tears pool in her eyes—tears she's too stubborn to shed. Her hands freeze in their task, and she drags in a sharp breath when she nods. Her entire body shudders for a moment as if her dead family did a collective sigh from the grave. And then, almost as if on their own accord, her fingers return to picking peas. "Know that not everyone hates John. Some wait for the opportunity to depose him. But others crave power for themselves. They'll seek any reason to unseat you as well. Your…situation…with Wren, Dax, and Quinn can be the perfect weapon to prove you are unfit to rule. They will call you wanton. Brand you a whore. Claim you are unworthy of the throne."

Each insult is a dagger to my heart. "Do you…" I can barely voice the question, the words a dry rasp that leave a bitter taste in my mouth as they tumble off my tongue. "Do you believe these things about me?"

Emma's expression softens. "No, Rapunzel, I do not." She leans in close. "I may even be a bit jealous of you if you want to know the truth." At her chuckle, I playfully swat her away. "In the time you've been here, I've seen into your heart. If I felt you were unfit to rule Rygard, I would toss you in a cage and throw away the key myself."

I believe she would.

Rygard deserves better than to replace a mortal tyrant with an indestructible one. And that might have been a genuine possibility if Sybil hadn't taken me as an infant. If John had raised me in his shadow, I might have become like him. Cruel. Unlike him, however, I can't easily be killed. Sybil's spell should have saved my dying mother's life while she was pregnant with me. Instead, the magic-infused my hair with…life.

My mother lived only as long as I was inside of her. The moment I took my first breath, my mother took her last. To protect me from my father, Sybil stole me. She cursed an entire forest and hid me deep in the heart of it. Locked me away inside a tower. And until three months ago, I hadn't known my father was a king.

"Promise me you'll be smart in how you conduct your affairs, Rapunzel."

I glanced at Dax and Quinn before shifting my attention back to Emma. "I promise we'll be careful."

"Good." She locks me in a fierce hug. "I feel like we've become sisters, and I fear for you."

I fear for myself, but this, I don't say aloud.

"I'll be fine, Emma." I set her at arm's length. "Do I seem frightened?" I'm positively terrified. "No, I don't. We're going to knock John off that throne, and once he's gone, I'll bring you to Newkirk to help me establish my court."

And maybe Queen Eleanor will stay after John is dead to be near her brother. With the rest of their family gone, they are all that's left of the Redgraves.

Together, we can defeat that son of a bitch, and when this is done…

Oh, God, when it's done.

Foremost, my goal is to be a good queen. But also to have what I never dreamed possible during those long and lonely years living in the tower.

A family of my own.

Chapter Five

WREN

"I'm going to miss this."

Quinn's admission shocks me, heard over the lively, and slightly off-tune, music. Arthur, his fingers flying over his gemshorn, and Kenric plucking away on a lute, have taken to entertaining us each evening since Rapunzel has breathed life into Dyhurst's ancient keep. And after she's learned a handful of dances, she's forced us to rush through supper so we can bring the instruments out.

I don't know where she finds the energy after a full day of training, but she does…

…because she's still catching up on what she missed during her lost years.

I give Quinn a healthy dose of side-eye. "Which part, Bryce's foul cooking or freezing your ass off in this drafty fortress?"

"All castles are drafty." He lifts a goblet of ale to his lips and takes a hearty swallow of the strong brew before gesturing to our small, makeshift family gathered in the hall. "And all of it, actually."

"Truth?" Tonight's meal of over-boiled potatoes and

scorched venison sits like a lump in my stomach. "I will as well."

A smirk tugs at his lips. "Imagine there was a time when you refused to even sit here." Quinn half-turns and raps his knuckles on the scarred surface of the long wooden table we're leaning against. "And share a meal with us."

The combined loss of my father and discovering the truth about John consumed me with rage. I was also still harboring a deep hatred for Rapunzel. Wrongly, I accused her of abandoning me when I needed her most. I didn't want to infect those around me with my bitterness.

"My anger did no one any good."

"You. Dax." Quinn pauses. "Me," he finally adds. "We've come far in a short time." He drags a hand through his long, black hair. "Something tells me it has everything to do with a pretty dancing pixie."

I follow Quinn's predatory gaze and locate Rapunzel in the center of the modest hall. She is a goddess in a yellow tunic. I can't pull my gaze from the enticing swell of her breasts above the dipped neckline as she dances a common carole along with Dax, Emma, Gavin, Bryce, and Lucian. Her laughter rises above the tune, more lyrical than any song a musician can play. And the longer I watch her, the less I see of the twelve-year-old I stumbled across a dozen years ago when she called down to me from her lone window at the top of her stark, gray tower. And yet, I still hear her melodic voice echo across that barren glade. Still remember the flutter in my belly when I caught my first glimpse of her.

And I still remember how afraid I was that she'd tumble to her death whenever she dangled her pretty little leg out that window.

When we met, I knew our lives would intertwine. What I hadn't realized was that the tower was our first obstacle. Not even our greatest. Maybe if I had known about Rapunzel's hair… But I hadn't. Nor had I known she felt its magic was a wall standing between us. She feared the power. Feared herself. Feared what others would do if they learned her hair could heal the sick and the dying. More than that, the enchanted strands protect her from harm. It keeps her alive. God forbid it gets cut…

I refuse to entertain the thought of losing her.

Quinn drains his goblet and slams it on the table behind us. "You had a reason for your anger."

Without acknowledging Quinn's remark, I keep my gaze trained on Rapunzel. She is radiant in Dax's arms—even when her feet tangle around themselves and she stumbles. For someone with such natural grace, our lady is inept at dancing. It's humorous to watch, and I catch myself outright laughing when Dax has to save her from herself many times.

"My anger was misguided," I admit with a shrug.

"Obviously all is forgiven," Quinn drawls.

"Obviously."

Quinn turns his back on the hall to refill his goblet. He presses one hand on the table, bracing himself, and angles his head to look at me. His black eyes remind me of an old, forgotten grave. "I worry about her, Wren. I don't like worrying about anyone. It feels… I don't fucking like it. And I sure as fuck don't want her at court alone."

His tension mirrors my own. Last thing I want is Rapunzel alone and vulnerable, but as much as I hate to admit it, her plan is sound. She's the one person who can get inside Newkirk without rousing suspicion. Once within the castle, she has the best chance of finding us a way in as well. Even if it's just Quinn. That's enough to kill John and end that bastard's barbaric reign.

"John is an ass." But unfortunately, the man is no fool. "He'll want her compliant. If, for nothing else, the optics of it when he presents her at court. And he *will* make a grand show of presenting his long-lost daughter to his courtiers. He'll have to,

Quinn. Too many people know he's tearing Rygard apart, searching for her. He can't risk harming even one hair on her lovely head."

My reasoning eases some of that tension in Quinn's shoulders. He knows I'm right. My father may have been John's closest friend, but Quinn's family—the Redgraves—were one step down from royalty. He was practically raised at Newkirk. If anyone knows John, he does. He understands John, although mad, is a controlled rage. He's ruthless, not reckless. As long as Rapunzel…behaves…she'll be safe.

But not indefinitely.

Eventually, he'll demand the use of her hair.

The plan is to kill him long before that happens.

Quinn spins back around to watch Rapunzel as she dances her way closer to us. A sneer curls his upper lip. "Too much can go wrong."

I wholeheartedly agree. And if there was any other way to get one of us inside Newkirk, I'd remove Rapunzel from this plan. But we've gone at this from all angles, and she can do what we can't. Quinn is, understandably, thinking with his heart and not his mind. With his younger sister, Eleanor, John's wife, I can't imagine her misery—and the added burden on Quinn's shoulders.

"We need to trust her, Quinn. As much as I hate this, she's the only one who can get us inside that fucking fortress."

Without taking his gaze off Rapunzel and Dax, Quinn clenches his jaw. His nod is slow, angry. "My sister… How much of her did that prick destroy?"

I give his shoulder a gentle squeeze. "If she's anything like you, John took nothing from her. Not one goddamn thing."

Quinn slides his black gaze my way, and in their dark depths I read his intentions like a book.

Vengeance.

Torment.

Murder.

"His death must be slow. Painful." His words are low and menacing. "I want him to hurt so badly, he'll take that pain with him to Hell."

"What you need to do is spend this time planning where you're going to display the bastard's heart after you rip it out of his chest."

Because one of the 'gifts' that came with Quinn's curse is the power to send a soul to Hell by…removing…their heart with his bare hands. True, it saps his strength and leaves him weak and vulnerable for days, but with someone like John, it's well worth the sacrifice.

Right then, Rapunzel strolls over, pulling Dax behind her. "What are you both conspiring about?"

Although it takes great effort, I resist the urge to kiss her pretty mouth. "Conspiring? Us? Nothing, my love."

She drops Dax's hand and wags a finger at me. "I know when you're up to something, Wren Kincaid."

"Do you?" I lift a single brow. "And how's that?"

"You're breathing," she quips with a *very* unladylike—but extremely adorable—snort.

Dax jerks his head at Emma. "You've been around that one too long."

Rapunzel laughs right in Dax's face. "You're sour because she's teaching me the advantages of being a woman."

Quinn rolls his eyes. "Fuck me, Rapunzel, but that's a load of horseshit."

She must take Quinn's words as a challenge because her demeanor changes. With an enticing sway of her shapely hips, she closes the short distance between them. Her slightly sun kissed hand, itself a paradox of fragility and strength, is a feather-light touch on Quinn's chest. When she slides her palm farther up his muscular pecs, then curves her fingers around his neck, it's me who can barely draw a breath. Standing on tiptoes, she leans forward until her lips brush his ear and purrs, "Odd, how you don't think it's horseshit when you have me on my knees."

Poor Quinn.

Rapunzel might as well put her face between his legs right here, right now. He slams his eyes shut. Squeezes them tight. Her words slither up the shaft of my cock, hardening it until it fills the crotch of my breeches to where I have to shift my stance.

"That wasn't nice," he grits out between clenched teeth. He opens his eyes, but keeps his hands fisted at his sides and his shoulders bunched. His sleeves are hitched to reveal the tattoos on his arms. They seem to stretch and constrict across his flesh in response to his arousal.

Slowly—so fucking slowly—Rapunzel removes her hand from his neck before she extends a finger to trace the jagged scar that slices down the left side of his face. "Another lesson you taught me." Her expression is positively licentious as she touches that same finger to her lips. The devious woman licks the pad with her talented tongue. "Never play nice."

"Keep it up, Princess." Quinn grabs her around the throat, pulling her closer. "I'll teach you another lesson. This one, with my cock in your mouth."

Dax and I exchange a meaningful glance at this erotic game of push and pull. And then Rapunzel gazes up at Quinn through the thick, sooty fringe of her lashes and discreetly cups him between the legs. "Promise?"

Quinn's low growl rumbles up from deep within his chest. "Be glad we're in a hall full of people."

"Why would I be glad when I enjoy being at your command? We," she motions to Wren, Dax, and herself, "know your pleasure is heightened not only by pain, but also by being watched. Same as Wren." She slides me a devious smile that sends a fresh wave of need rushing through me. "And Dax enjoys a bit of playfulness." Then she scans the room and seems satisfied that we're being ignored as the music continues and Emma and Gavin are dancing while everyone else chats amongst themselves. "Seems I'll have to make this an early night."

"Bold of you to think I'll make it easy for you," he counters.

She shuffles backward a step, their extraordinary tug of war still going strong. "I wouldn't dare presume such a thing."

A malicious gleam lights Quinn's eyes. "You're going to have work for my cock tonight."

"Challenge accepted, Quinn." Rapunzel drags in a trembling breath. "I'll work for your cock." She flicks her gaze to his crotch before drifting back to his face. "But not before one last dance. Come, Wren. Let him watch us and imagine all the wicked things he wants to do to me."

Rapunzel's little hand slides against mine, and as she drags me away from Quinn and Dax, I issue her a warning. "You're playing with fire, Zee."

"But what a lovely way to burn." When she comes to a stop, she wraps her arms around my neck. Her smirk is downright devious. She steps up on her tiptoes and puts her lips to my ear. "I'll tell you a secret, Wren. I do enjoy the rush of baiting him."

I laugh at her confession. "Fuck me, but we've created a monster."

"Oh, no, Wren." Rapunzel stumbles a bit while struggling to execute the steps to the Basse Dance. "Make no mistake about it. You may have freed me, but you didn't create the monster. All you did was let her out of her tower."

So I did.

Three months ago, when I dragged her out. What Rapunzel doesn't realize is that she wasn't the only one liberated that day.

I set myself free as well.

RAPUNZEL

"*Two truths to redeem his soul.*"

The demon's angry voice slices my mind from one ear to the other. A hot dagger that stabs its way across my skull. It's a painful, guttural murmur only I hear. Words I can't escape fill my ears. My eyelids fly open, freeing me from the nightmare that held me in its grip. The whisper follows me into consciousness. Once awake, I'm still kept locked in the demon's clutches. Its evil eyes hold me captive. Suffocating and paralyzing. I try to scream for Wren, but my voice is stuck somewhere in the back of my throat. When I attempt to lift my arms, they're weighted against the mattress, too heavy to lift. My limbs are banded to the bed by invisible restraints that render me helpless.

Vulnerable.

"*Cease your struggles, Rapunzel of Rygard.*" As if I have a choice but to comply. The creature robbed me of movement. Of my voice. My hand itches for my sword, but I'm powerless to do anything other than lie here and wait.

Wait for him to… What? Take my soul like he did Quinn's?

The demon steps from the shadows. Its massive body blocks the moonlight that filters in from the recessed lead-glass windows. How could I have forgotten how horrifying this creature is? How massive? Its ebony horns nearly scrape the ceiling. Gray skin is stretched taut over thick cords of muscle. Its flesh bears the same vine-like markings as Quinn's. When it purses thin lips and spits on the floor, strings of thick saliva hang from its fangs.

"Fuck your soul. I have no need of it."

Then what does it want because I have nothing else to offer?

"But I do have a proposition, Rapunzel of Rygard."

My initial instinct shouts *no* inside my mind, but curiosity overrules reason.

"Two truths to free your precious Quinn," the demon hisses, with its breath reeking of rotting flesh.

Excitement and confusion clash on the heels of revulsion. The demon trails its claw down my right cheek and across the curve of my jawline to my exposed collarbone that peeks from above the yellow blanket. Vomit flows up my throat, but I swallow it with my scream. The demon smirks at me, obviously enjoying my fear. Is this how it was for Quinn when he bartered away his soul? Was he as helpless?

Afraid?

Desperate?

"Yes, and more."

Oh, God…

"God has no part in this transaction."

I faced this beast the day I saved Quinn's life. That terror comes back in a violent wave that threatens to drown me. But the demon's hold prevents me from sinking under the tide. It keeps my eyes wide open, focused on its hideous face, black eyes, and razored teeth.

"He has…lost his appeal." The demon is angry. As if Quinn cheated him. *"But a bargain was made."* It leans in too close. Its

foul breath makes my eyes water. Or am I crying over the possibility of Quinn's redemption? *"Two truths freely confessed and sealed in blood. Coerce him, and I'll rip out his intestines and shove them down your throat."*

I'd nod if I could. Drop to my knees and scream my acquiescence. But I can't. Instead, I think it so loudly I'm surprised Wren doesn't wake from the force of my thoughts.

Wren.

I attempt to turn my head to check to see if the demon hasn't harmed him.

Again, it reads my mind and cackles as if dealing with a fool. *"Your dear Wren sleeps peacefully at your side, Rapunzel of Rygard."*

My gratitude for Wren's safety and the joy that this creature is giving Quinn a second chance both die swift deaths because I remember a bitter lesson life has taught me.

Nothing comes without a price.

The demon tilts its head, and I cringe when those claws come dangerously back toward my face. I even squeeze my eyes shut, but they fly open when he runs them through my hair. *"A single strand. That's my price."*

One strand of my hair?

This must be demon trickery.

"No trick, future queen of Rygard. I do not play fast and loose with bargains." Its mouth curls into a sneer as it lifts a lock of my hair. I don't want it touching me. It's…vulgar. And it must know I don't want its hands on any part of me because those malevolent eyes bore into me with such hubris. Such challenge. It knows I won't deny it anything, not with the fate of Quinn's soul hanging in the balance.

The demon wraps the golden strands around its gnarled fingers. *"One taste is what I desire in exchange for freeing Quinn Redgrave's soul."*

"Agree or no?"

Agree!

Of course, I agree. I agree a hundred times over and would give up so much more.

My acceptance is barely a finished thought when, with the flick of a finger, the demon seizes his prize. His release of my body is instant. I suck in a hard breath, quiet, mindful not to wake Wren. I exhale on a trembling breath and squeeze my eyes closed, with agony flowing through me in blinding waves.

I choke back my sob because, my God, severing even one length of hair feels like the hack of a limb. The demon towers over me, and when I crack open my eyes, I see it relishing my pain—*absorbing* it. It licks its lips with a red, forked tongue like my agony is its favorite flavor. And while I fight not to writhe lest I wake Wren, the demon tucks that strand into its mouth, its eyes rolling back in their sockets.

Finally, the creature smiles at me, a gross, perverted form of a grin, and releases a groan that rumbles from deep within its chest. It even has the audacity to cup between its legs, rubbing itself with sucking in ecstasy.

Wren stirs beside me, but the demon, with the word. *"Hush,"* returns him to his deep sleep. Then to me, it says, *"Your innocence is divine. A worthy exchange. Our bargain is complete. Two truths, freely offered, sealed in blood. Upon completion, I shall relinquish Quinn Redgrave's soul and return it to him. The terms of our pact fulfilled."*

A single tear of gratitude slips from the outer corner of my eye.

Thank you.

My appreciation screams inside my mind even as the demon laughs in my face. *"Foolish woman. When he's no longer mine, he'll be your problem to tame."*

And that's why I smile when the demon vanishes into the shadows. Quinn now unknowingly has hope of escaping an eternity of torment in hell, but he also doesn't need to be tamed. He is perfect as he is.

Wild.

Wonderful.

Free.

Mine.

Chapter Seven

WREN

The skittish buck hears it before I do.

With a flick of its ears, the animal rears its head. Scans the area, then takes off, running deeper into the forest.

Fuck.

I'm instantly on alert and shift my attention—and loaded bow—to the speckled brown steed charging toward me. Silently cursing, I focus on the man guiding the galloping horse. In my peripheral vision, I watch our meal disappear into the trees. The sunlight filtering in through the autumn leaves gives the illusion that the forest is on fire. I remain crouched and ready to impale the person foolish enough to infringe on our quiet corner of Rygard. But shaggy blonde curls tell me it's Ian, and I relax my stance and un-notch the arrow.

I rise from the brush to reveal myself and give a wave. Ian offers nothing back.

Fuuuck.

Something's wrong.

Gripping the horse's reins with one hand, he's holding his

side with the other. The closer he gets, the worse he looks. His hair hangs matted to his sweaty face. His expression contorted with pain. The animal skids to a stop next to me, with Ian's shallow panting worrying me as much as the blood staining his torn brown tunic.

"I followed them, Wren," Ian grits out. He blinks long and hard before pulling his hand from the blood-crusted wound. "Followed them for days. All the way to Blythe Forest."

The bow and arrow fall forgotten from my fingers at his announcement. "What?"

Ian swallows. Drags in a hard breath. "Aye." He nods slowly. Sways in the saddle, his lips twisted in a rueful grin. "With the princess gone, the curse… It's lifted."

Lifted? The fuck? A flood of questions rips through my mind, with the loudest one being… Does this mean Sybil is dead? Christ. If so, it will destroy Rapunzel.

But I push all those questions aside as I help Ian off his horse. The moment his feet touch the ground, his knees buckle, and he collapses in a heap. Loyal to its rider, his horse takes a few steps back but stays close, acting as a sentry.

Following Ian down, I crouch beside my friend and try to keep my expression neutral even as I glimpse the wound that slashes up his side. "What happened?"

Ian bites the fingertips of his worn leather gloves to pull them off. Dried blood flakes off them and freckles his face. "The soldiers." He gulps for more air. "They found the tower. Oh, God, Wren. They saw me following them." He drags in another breath, then grimaces. "Water, please. I need water."

"Of course." With a leap to my feet, I dash to where I left my supplies and grab my waterskin. I hurry back, uncorking it as I go. Hand it to him, then angle him up in my arms. Ian drinks it fast, gulping it down until he coughs. "Easy, brother."

He nods, coughing some more before drinking slower. When

he hands it back to me, he heaves a rumbling sigh. One that troubles me because it's a sound I've heard too many times on the battlefield.

It's the death rattle.

"I felled two of the bastards, but they got me." Ian's words are a struggle. "They got me good." He cringes when he touches his ruined side. There's so much dried blood staining his shredded shirt. "Those fuckers left me for dead, but you know me. Stubborn as a mule." He gives me a bloody grin. "I had to die on my terms."

With Ian propped up on my lap, I nod as I fight back a surge of heartbreak and anger. "You're home now, and we need to get you inside."

"Wren." Right when I'm about to move him, Ian grabs my wrist. "They're on the king's orders to resume a path of destruction until they find Princess Rapunzel."

Goddamnit.

We knew this reprieve of peace wouldn't last, but we hoped to have more time. More time to train Rapunzel—and more time to love her. But fucking John and his greed and insatiable quest for power. Knowing Rapunzel, she won't hide away here while her father destroys this kingdom hunting her. Nor is it my right, or Quinn and Dax's, to stop her.

Victory at any cost.

That's how John lives. To defeat him, we taught Rapunzel to think that way as well. But the lesson is nasty, and I'm finding it difficult to accept right now when it's my friend dying in my arms.

"Don't worry about that. Right now, our greatest concern is getting you inside Dyhurst." Because Ian's made it this far. He deserves to die on Dyhurst soil, surrounded by his family. I hook an arm under him and carefully—so damn carefully—help him to his feet. But he's all weakened limbs and shallow breathing. "I got you. Lean on me."

Fury and anguish clash violently, and I must battle them back as I take Ian's considerable weight. He's a big man. Tall. Brawny. He stumbles when he comes down on me, and we nearly buckle but quickly recover and find our footing. Then it's an amble past his horse. I contemplate hoisting him onto the saddle, but there's no way I can easily lift this mountain of a man on that animal without further damaging him. Even this movement has him bleeding anew, so with a light slap on the steed's hindquarters, I send it racing home.

For us, it's a grueling trudge toward the castle.

Thankfully, I hadn't ventured far for today's hunt. Still, it's a slow trudge, with him needing to take rests to catch his breath. Each time we stop, he grows weaker. His resumed pace is more sluggish. The moment Gavin spots us from his station atop the parapet, he shouts for the gate to be opened. We lumber inside to controlled chaos charging toward us, and it's much like when Quinn nearly died all over again. Flashbacks of that awful fucking day haunt me as I drag Ian into Dyhurst's courtyard. The gate slams behind us right as Quinn reaches us. He sweeps Ian up, with Rapunzel already calling for her 'supplies.' From the arduous trek, Ian's wound leaks a trail of blood in our wake as he's carried toward the keep. But by the time Quinn sits Ian in a wingback chair near the hearth, I fear it's already too late. That Ian has already lost too much blood…

…until Rapunzel shoves through everyone. Bryce hands her a satchel that contains three smaller bags of herbs. It also contains shears and a mortar and pestle. Everything she needs to save a life—and cut time off hers. She collects her skirt in one hand, about to drop to her knees and get to work, but Ian stops her.

"Princess, no," he rasps.

The material spills from her grasp. She places a hand on his arm. "Let me do this for you."

Ian pats her hand, but weak, his arm flops to his side. He

turns his head to focus his watery gaze on the flames flickering in the hearth. "I'm tired, Princess. I'm tired of mourning my wife and child." He lets his glazed stare roam to each of us before settling back on Rapunzel. "I did my part. I told Wren John's plan. Now I need to be with my Margaret and Beatrice." He lifts a dirty, trembling finger, pointing at nothing. His bloody grin is filled with heartrending joy. "Can you see them? Can you see how beautiful they are? As lovely as when I last saw them."

With silent tears raining down her face, Rapunzel returns her satchel to Bryce. "I don't need this." She kneels and gently strokes Ian's hand, nodding. "Yes, Ian, I see them." Her voice is calming. Soothing. Even to me. Everyone follows suit and gets on their knees. We all gather around a dear friend to witness his soul break free from the limitations of life. From the horrors of having our families taken from us. From the agony of having to continue living when what we are living for is dead.

Rapunzel's hand falls away from Ian's, and she dabs tears from the corners of her eyes. "Your family is beautiful." Then she glances at the empty place where Ian was pointing. "You are lovely together."

When she turns back to Ian, she hitches in a breath when she sees he's died.

Everyone around him is also quietly weeping or on the verge of tears.

All these goddamn tears. All this sorrow. This needless death. Caused by one man.

And for what?

For what goddamn reason did John cause this anguish?

How dare he take and take and take without ever facing the consequences of his greed and cruelty? How dare he cause this destruction and continue to live?

When John murdered my father, he didn't just kill his friend. He signed his death warrant. The day is fast approaching when we'll put that son of a bitch in the fucking dirt where he belongs. Until then, I shove aside the burning need for revenge to lay Ian to rest.

Because tomorrow…

Tomorrow it's time to leave Dyhurst.

Chapter Eight

RAPUNZEL

Still rattled from my encounter with the demon and distraught after losing Ian, I sit atop my gray mare with a morning mist promising a long, miserable day. Although I understand why we must go, I selfishly want to stay. It took Wren less than two years to bring us together and breathe life into Dyhurst. I fell in love with this ancient fortress the moment it came into view the day they brought me here. Every person who lives within its decaying walls has become my family.

I wasn't ready to say goodbye.

Rygard seems to weep along with me. Dax, understandably somber, is beside me on a brown steed—the same one we rode in on when they brought me here.

My mare, such a polite lady, waits patiently. Dax's horse stomps its front feet, pawing at the mud while Wren issues his final instructions to those who stay behind. And Quinn… Quinn is off doing something else. He has been more grim than usual since we put Ian in the ground.

Dax soothes his restless mount, and I marvel over how patient and kind he is toward the animal.

When I hunker deeper into the cloak draped around my shoulders, Dax notices. "Cold?"

I shake my head. "I'm quite warm, actually."

Just heartbroken and anxious.

The gusting wind hits like a bitter slap, but it's true. I hardly feel it, nestled as I am under my layers of clothing. Wren insisted I forgo a gown in favor of men's garb. Scandalous, sure, but functional. Being stuck in a saddle is more comfortable when wearing breeches than a skirt. Emma stitched my clothes together in preparation for this journey. The brown linen shirt, wool jerkin, and cloak keep out the chill. The thick fur-lined cloak over it, though, makes all the difference. Still, being out in the rain, with the hood pulled up over my head, it's already damp.

With my hands tucked into leather gloves and my braided hair stuffed safely hidden under my clothes, it's concealed. A necessity since we're unsure how much the outside world has learned about me. Not that we suspect John told many people about my existence, but still... Rumors spread, and there's too much land between Dyhurst and Newkirk for unnecessary risks. Best not to draw unwanted attention during our trek.

"Your face is red from the cold already." Dax is close enough to lean over and run his knuckles down the bridge of my runny nose. Unlike me, he's not wrapped up tight. Nor does he seem affected by the chill that must permeate his breeches, leather jerkin, and wool cloak. The hood is loose over his head, more hanging off than covering him against the annoying mist. "You're going to freeze to death before we get to Newkirk."

"It's October, not February," I remind him, although his concern is sweet. "I'll survive."

He motions to my mare with a jut of his chin. "Let's see what you say after a full day sitting in that saddle with the wind slapping at your face."

"Are you trying to frighten me, Dax Stafford?"

"He doesn't need to try," Quinn drawls as he strolls from the keep. Dressed head to foot in black, he is a living shadow. He moves with incredible grace for a man of his height and muscular physique—a testimony to a lifetime spent wielding a sword. And while he, like Dax, is always worried about my well-being, he's not obviously concerned for himself. At least the stubborn man finally pulls the hood of his wool cloak over his head.

One hand rests on the pommel of his sword. In the other, he carries a satchel that's nearly full to bursting. When he reaches his black steed, he takes a moment to give the incredibly well-trained animal a gentle scratch behind its ear. "You should be fucking terrified."

"Well, I'm not." I lift my chin and match his glare. "This day marks a new beginning for this kingdom."

He narrows those dark eyes on me. Dare I admit to seeing pride in them?

"Good." After securing the pouch to the saddle, Quinn mounts his steed. His ebony hair hangs free around his face. The dark, wild strands brush his broad shoulders, giving him a primal edge that takes my breath away. When he pulls the hood of his black cloak over his head, it hides the sharp features of his face, swallowing his somber expression in shadow. "Don't you dare forget what we're setting out to accomplish."

I swallow the lump that's jumped up—and gotten stuck—in the back of my throat. "Victory at any cost."

"I've already lost one woman I…care about…to that fucking piece of shit. Don't let him take you from me as well," Quinn mutters. I'm not sure if it's meant for me to hear, but I did—and so does my heart. Then he motions to the satchel. "Bryce packed us enough food to last a month, at least."

That has Dax smiling. "Can't say I won't appreciate a taste of home while on the road."

"Let's see what you say when we're gnawing on stale bread

and grinding our teeth on venison that's tougher to chew than leather." Then Quinn turns to me and…stares. Watches for so long, I bristle under his scrutiny.

Shifting in the saddle, I gather the fur-lined cloak tighter around myself. Finally, when I can't take his silent stare for one more moment. I tilt my head and shrug my shoulders. "Is something amiss?"

"Not at this moment." Still, he doesn't take his gaze from me. "I am a man appreciating his woman."

Untucking a hand, I swipe errant wisps of hair the drizzle has stuck to my forehead. "I am a drowned rat."

"You are captivating." Quinn's midnight gaze wanders over me. "What I can see of you, anyway, buried as you are." And then his mouth—those wicked lips that bring me such pleasure—lift in the hint of a grin. "Not that it matters how many layers you wear. I know what's underneath."

"Can't have her catch her death." Dax makes a dramatic shudder as if the cold is suddenly too much for him.

Quinn pulls a sardonic face. "Call it a hunch, but I doubt the elements will cause Rapunzel to catch her death."

Along with healing and keeping me alive, my hair also maintains my health. It prevents me from falling ill. I've never even experienced something as common as the sniffles.

Dax opens his mouth to speak but snaps his mouth closed when Wren emerges from the keep. He strides toward us, bow in hand and quiver full of arrows slung over his back. His chestnut hair is pulled away from his face and tied at the nape of his neck. With his expression as bleak as the morning, he says nothing as he greets his majestic brown steed with a scratch under its chin. The animal nudges him for more affection, and he complies by kissing the sweet beast on the side of the head before mounting.

Then he heaves out a loud and long sigh. "Ready?"

Quinn nods. "As ever we'll be."

Wren gives me a curt nod. I offer him a small, reassuring

smile in answer. Then Dax spurs his horse into motion, and my stomach seems to fall to my feet. This day was inevitable. Eventually, we had to leave this desolate, crumbling castle. But as Hope, my sweet, speckled gray, takes her first steps to carry me toward my future, I don't want to go. Selfishly, I want to hop off her back and run straight inside the keep.

Odd, I spent twenty-four years as a voluntary prisoner inside a tower, yet it was never my home. But Dyhurst… It's become my haven, and when I glance over my shoulder and see it behind me, the sting of tears catches me by surprise.

Wren drops back to ride beside me. "Zee?"

"I'm fine, Wren." I stare ahead because if I look at him, I'll break. "I can do this."

Dax falls in step on my left, his horse snorting as if it wants to run wild through the trees. "We know you can, Little Captive."

I grip the reins as if my life depends on it, apprehension and determination leaving no room for fear. "John will burn Rygard until he finds me." Finally, I look at Wren, and I see it… A word from me, and he'll turn right back and take me home. Unacceptable. "Every death will be on my conscience. I could never live with that."

"No, you couldn't."

His quiet agreement reminds me so much of the little boy he was, who would visit me day after day, month after month, for eight years, desperately trying to convince me I had the courage to leave the tower. I never dared to believe him—until the day that soldier murdered his mother and pushed him too far. On that day, something changed in both of us. That day, he wouldn't be denied when I refused to leave. But that day…

That day, I finally believed I was strong enough to leave my prison.

And today—this day—I know I'm strong enough to defeat a king.

"There is only one death I want on my conscience," I whisper, and for a moment, I fear I spoke so low, no one but Quinn could hear me.

But Wren says, "Then get us into Newkirk so we can help you do it and put the fucking crown on your head."

Chapter Nine

QUINN

Took long enough, but the early morning drizzle finally gave way to the afternoon sun. With the clouds gone, the dry, warmer weather makes our trek across the rugged southwest corner of Rygard somewhat pleasant, given the circumstances. The goal is to get to Lansing by midday tomorrow. It'll take hard riding, and truth be known, I expected Rapunzel to have a few complaints by now.

She proved me wrong.

We've been traveling for hours, stopping only once—briefly —to stretch our legs and devour a quick meal. Then it was back in the saddle and on our way, whipping wind and all, to maximize the daylight.

The combination of damp clothes and sitting all damn day in a fucking saddle chaffed my balls. So much for my unholy healing ability. The constant friction negates the expedited recovery process. I blame John for this discomfort, of course. We shouldn't be here. We should be at Dyhurst. I should be on the lists enjoying a leisurely afternoon beating the shit out of Wren or Dax. Preferably Dax. Instead, my balls are cold and chaffed. We'll be sleeping on the ground, freezing our asses off rather than tucked into a warm bed after an evening spent fucking Rapunzel.

I don't even get to ride alongside her. That pleasure is Wren and Dax's, the lucky bastards. Their duty is to protect her. My function is to protect us *all*. I see what they can't. Hear what they don't. I'll detect a threat long before they can. Therefore, it's my job to take the lead. I've occasionally dropped back, though. I had the privilege of viewing Rygard through Rapunzel's fascinated eyes each time I did.

How she adores this land.

While at Dyhurst, I had a false sense of isolation. The months there made our war with John deceptively personal when, in fact, this entire kingdom will suffer should we fall.

Failure, however, is not an option.

John is already dead.

We just haven't killed him yet.

Now that we've cantered past the twin towns of Leighton Falls and Haversville—the latter of which is still being rebuilt after John's soldiers destroyed it months ago— I relax a bit. I nearly died there and can still taste the fucking poison from that tainted blade that slid across my throat. But we're in open terrain now, and I scan the distance, detecting no threat. The occasional curious critter scampers by, and although I can catch them and make a meal of them, I feel benevolent. We'll make do with the provisions Bryce provided us. I'll let those animals live another day.

With the sun just now beginning its descent and Turner Forest still far off, I maintain a quick pace. Last thing we need is to get caught out in the open come nightfall. We'll camp in the woods, then do a hard push in the morning for Lansing Village. The Cup and Crown is the halfway point between Dyhurst and Newkirk Castle. Although Rapunzel is nervous about meeting Dax's mother, we'll rest at her tavern for the night and replenish our supplies before making another relentless drive for John's court in the northeast corner of Rygard.

With one ear on the surrounding landscape to listen for impending danger, I keep the other on the quiet conversation behind me. Rapunzel's melodic voice soothes me. Quiets the constant rage simmering within me. She is sunlight to my darkness, and while she'd likely claim it has all to do with the magic of her hair, she'd be wrong. The woman herself is a marvel. Serene. Brave. Capable and determined.

Stubborn to a fault.

Rapunzel is everything I never thought I deserved but silently wished for.

"…if she hates me?"

I catch the tail end of Rapunzel's question, and I tilt my head to better hear what's said between her, Dax, and Wren.

"Adele Stafford hates almost everyone, but she'll love you," Dax assures her.

The ornery woman has the temper of a dragon, but with family, Adele has quite the soft spot.

"How can you be sure? She doesn't know me. What if she hates me because of my father?" Rapunzel presses Dax.

"Adele will love you because her son loves you," Wren drawls, and I nearly choke on my spit.

Love.

Now that's a drastic fucking word. One I spoke only to my family, and even then, I said it occasionally at most. It's a word that, if I'm being honest, has been a needle in the back of my mind these last few weeks whenever I think about Rapunzel. I've even had to swallow it down a time or two, lest it foolishly tumbles from lips in sudden moments of weakness.

The tension emanating from Rapunzel hits my back like an icy wave. Her words are a cautious whisper. So low even I can barely hear them. "Our…*arrangement…* Emma warned me others might find it…unseemly. I'm afraid your mother will think me wanton. Perhaps even a disgrace."

That last word damn near splits my miserable heart in two.

Of course, we'll need to keep our relationship private for Rapunzel's reputation. I never considered how this might affect her. The stress of it now that she's away from Dyhurst.

"Never," Dax promises her. "My mother thumbs her nose at societal rules. Trust me, Rapunzel, she will not give one fuck about what we do behind closed doors. She will love you."

What Dax doesn't do is counter Wren's claim that he is in love with Rapunzel. The tender accusation hangs over us when I slow my mount to fall in step with them. Only Rapunzel's windburned face is visible from beneath her bundle of clothing. The sparkle in her eyes when she looks at me punches me right in the goddamn gut.

"Adele knows a good person when she meets one," I assure Rapunzel.

Her little shrug is barely perceptible from beneath all those layers. "She might feel compelled to like me because—"

"The devil himself cannot force my mother to do a damn thing against her will." Dax says, cutting off Rapunzel. "Now, cease working yourself up into a worry."

Rapunzel chews her inner cheek a moment before lifting her chin in a charming display of courage. In this moment, even with her cheeks ruddy and her body hidden beneath a merchant shop's worth of fabric, it's easy to imagine Rygard's crown sitting atop her lovely head. She is regal. There's a gentle majesty in the way she holds herself. No amount of years in the tower could temper the nobility out of her.

"And I shall adore her." A hint of a smile curls her lips, and her heartbeat races a moment before she sighs out the confession, "With the same love and loyalty I have for her son."

Dax's rush of joy flows around us like a ribbon, and for one jealous moment, I wish it were me she professed that love for.

And as quickly as that ridiculous desire was born, it dies a terrible death. My life never allowed for affairs of the heart, and while I enjoy what I have with Rapunzel, I don't pretend it's on par with what she shares with Wren or Dax.

They aren't…broken.

Soulless.

Damned.

They can give her something I never can.

A future.

Chapter Ten

QUINN

"Quinn?"

My spine stiffens at Rapunzel whispering my name like it's the sweetest song. I slide my eyes closed, the cold water lapping at my stomach. The vine-like tattoos on my torso, arms, and hands—visual reminders of my deal with the demon—tighten across my flesh. As if they're reacting for her, desperate for a taste of her.

Rapunzel should be asleep. Tucked away safely in her bedroll by the fire. Instead, she's here, standing behind me on the bank of the river. I can smell her all around me.

I reopen my eyes and turn to look at her…

…the woman is a vision in the moonlight. A goddess among mortals, with her golden hair hanging free around her tiny body. The long, thick mass appears almost silvery under the pale glow. Watching me, she looks too serious by half. And her eyes… Fuck. Those luminous gems. Her gaze is a more tangible touch against my naked flesh than the water lapping at my waist.

"Why aren't you sleeping, Princess?"

She gathers the brown cloak tighter around herself and steps closer to where the river rolls up the bank. Her bare feet leave tiny imprints in the mud, and I'm about to scold her for not wearing shoes because her toes must be damn near frozen. "My mind won't allow it."

Her hushed confession kills my castigation as I listen to Wren returning to our camp. "You're here alone. Why?"

When she licks her lips, it's a phantom touch that sears me. "There are things that need to be said." She takes another step, her toes now in the water. One hand pokes out from the seam where the folds of her cloak meet when she gestures to me and then to herself. "Between us."

Raking my fingers through my hair to push the wet strands from my face, I stalk from the river. The way Rapunzel's eyes graze my body warms me more than the lash of the sun's rays in the heart of summer. In the quiet of the night, her soft sign whispers so loudly. Her heart hammers a frantic beat as I stride toward her and when she backs out of the water and blinks those wide, enchanting eyes at me.

I swear on all that's holy, I almost remember what it's like to have a soul.

Almost.

"No, Rapunzel, there's nothing we need to say."

I'm no fool. Rapunzel believes she's riding toward her death, and this is her wanting to say her goodbyes. To make sure we leave nothing unspoken.

Heedless of the cold, I cup her chin and capture her gaze. "Whatever you need to tell me can wait until after Rygard's crown is safely on your head." I brush my lips over hers. "Do you understand what I'm telling you, Rapunzel?"

"Yes." Her hesitant whisper nearly breaks me.

"That's my good girl." I stroke her hair, finding how she leans into my touch precious. I trail my hand lower until I have a firm hold on her throat. Her rapid pulse against my palm feeds my excitement. I squeeze just enough to cut off her air. To ignite sparks of green fire in her eyes. Enough to help her forget why we're here. "Let's test your obedience, shall we?"

"You think I'm frightened?" Rapunzel raises her chin. "I dare you, Quinn. Test me. Do it. I've had excellent teachers."

After a quick scan of the surrounding forest to ensure we're safe, I turn my predatory stare back on Rapunzel and give her a slow, purposeful appraisal. "What's about to happen here will make the devil turn away in shock."

She swallows hard against my grip. "The things you say—"

"Make you ache for my cock," I finish for her. A flush darkens her cheeks. "Go ahead, Princess. Deny it. I dare *you*. Even if your words lie for you, your body doesn't." The frantic rhythm of her heartbeat fills my ears. "I smell the desire on you."

"I do like it," she confesses on a whimper. "Oh, God, Quinn, I like it too much."

My wild spirit and her need for freedom collide. They whip into a frenzy. Grow into a blaze that spreads. It quickly becomes an inferno—that inferno threatening to consume us both.

Her touch makes the world fade, with the trees, dirt, moon, and the whispering sounds of the forest suddenly so distant. Even the demon's perpetual grim and haunting presence disappears. Right now, all that matters is Rapunzel.

So small.

Delicate.

So fucking mine.

"Can you hear it, Quinn?" She rests her hands on my bare hips, but it's a lightning strike right to the tip of my hard cock.

I always hear so much. *Too* much. It's why I traded my soul. My heightened senses allow me to hear Wren and Dax's conversation as if I were sitting among them despite the distance between us. The thundering of her heart and the rush of blood through her veins. "Hear what, Rapunzel?"

"Rygard. It calls to me."

I release her throat to grab her ass over the cloak. Pull her close and grind my cock against her stomach. Lean in to press my lips to the sensitive shell of her ear. Rub my cheek against her hair, with her silken strands catching on the stubble of my beard. "All I hear is you."

Her purposeful little fingers kneed at me. "I've heard the voice of this kingdom all my life, like a whisper in my mind, but never realized it was Rygard." She reaches up to cup the nape of my neck, sending chills down my spine. "I never understood what it told me until Wren took me from the tower."

I lean back to stare into her storied eyes. "And what does it tell you, Rapunzel?"

"That I'm stronger than a mighty king."

"What about a soulless man?" I graze her sensitive neck with my lips before I sink my teeth into her sweet flesh, pulling a gasp from her. "Are you stronger than me, Princess?"

"We all have different strengths. You taught me that. But tonight." Rapunzel drops her head back to give me better access to her throat. "Tonight, I'm whatever you need me to be."

"Smart answer." My eye catches on the silver pommel of my freshly washed sword. Then I look back at her, mesmerized by her courage and beauty. Always so eager to experience pleasure. To teeter on the edge of pain. With an arrogant grin, I leave her to retrieve my sword. "Let's see how beautiful you are when the limits of your obedience are tested."

Her eyes whip to the weapon, her brows furrowing in question. "Quinn…?"

Each rapid beat of her heart betrays her trepidation. Every hard swallow is fascinating as she fights for courage. How brave of her. How wonderfully captivating—and utterly reckless in her quest to experience everything in life. Everything that I want to give her.

"You trust me," I remind her. "Unconditionally."

She's already nodding before I finish speaking. "Uncondi-tionally," she breathes.

The cloak slides down her body like a second skin, puddling around her feet. She stands before me, delightfully tempting in a white shirt and breeches.

Moonlight glints off the blade as I run my index finger along the pristine metal. With a turn of my wrist, I grip the flat of the sharpened steel. I gesture at her with a nod of my chin. "Take off those breeches before I cut them off you."

Needing no further coaxing, Rapunzel does as I command. Then she widens her stance to give me unfettered access to her sex. The little imp even lifts her shirt to bare her lower body to my greedy gaze. The whisper of a cool breeze prickles her skin. But the slide of my sword's pommel up her pale inner thigh causes her to shiver. It's enthralling, the image of my weapon against such pure flesh. And when she squeezes her eyes closed against the decadent sensation of cold metal, I hook a finger under her chin.

"Eyes on me, Princess." I tease the hilt higher, closer to the juncture of her thighs. "I want you to watch me while I fuck you with my sword."

I live by the blade, and one day I'll likely die by it. Death and destruction collide each time I pull this sword from its sheath. To me, it's an extension of my body, and after tonight, when I hold it in my hand, I'll feel this moment against my palm.

Her moan echoes on the quiet night as her lids slowly lift. When I drag the simple, round pommel along her soaked slit, evidence of her arousal streaks the handle. She rises onto her tiptoes. As if I'll allow her to escape what I'm about to do.

"Keep your feet flat on the ground." I tease her bottom lip with a little bite. "You'll take what I give you like a good girl, Rapunzel." I snake an arm around her waist, with my palm pressed to the small of her back. "Disobedience isn't an option."

She comes down off her toes and releases a strained, ragged breath. "Please."

"Please what, Princess?" I lick the seam of her mouth,

relishing her sweet flavor. "You enjoy it when I hurt you." To prove this, I push the pommel in just enough to give her a sample of the relentless steel. "Do you know why?"

"Yes."

"Tell me," I growl.

She's exquisitely vulnerable. Raw. I burn this moment deep in my mind to take with me to Hell. "It makes me *feel*." She hitches in a whimper. "When you touch me…your hands, they make me forget what it felt like when I was numb." I reward her honesty with another slow tease of the sword's pommel along her cunt. She rocks her hips, chasing the steel. "More."

"Then get on your back and open those pretty legs nice and wide for me."

I don't have to tell her twice.

Rapunzel pulls her shirt over her head and tosses it aside before falling to the dirt. What a sight she is, bathed in the pale glow of the moon with her glorious golden hair spread out around her. I drop to my knees in the space between her spread calves. With my hand carefully closed around the sword's blade, I part her lips and torment her with the pommel.

She arches her back. Wriggles her hips. "Please, Quinn. I need…"

"I know what you fucking need." I push the pommel in just a little. To give her a taste of what's coming.

Her hips shoot right off the dirt to capture more of the steel. She throws her arms wide and rakes her fingers through the dirt, whimpering. Keeps her eyes locked on me. They're alive with excitement as I give the sword a slight twist. "That's evil," she gasps.

"You *do* know who I am." I lean forward, brace my weight on one arm, and drop my head to kiss her hard. Plunge my tongue into her mouth and swallow her next groan before grinding against her lips, "Take a deep breath." At my instruction, she gulps in the crisp air. "Keep those legs apart, or I'll bind your ankles and tie them to a tree to force them open."

The threat works. Her obedience feeds the feral side of me that craves depravity in all its bloody glory. That needs to skate along the edge where pain melts into pleasure and life meets death.

Rapunzel, trembling from the cold and pleasure, is fucking exquisite. She's soaked, wetting the way for the steel as I feed in more. Her body stretches, accepting the ruthless hilt until her pussy swallows the pommel. I savor her every breath and moan, intoxicated by her pleasure as I push in deeper. Slowly. Allow her body to accommodate the metal. Rub the handle's cold, unyielding definition along her warm and tender walls.

"So fucking beautiful," I rasp. "Every time my hand is on my sword, I'll remember your cunt wrapped around it."

I claim her mouth, dominating her. Demanding all she has to give. Everything she is—and then more. I work her pussy with a slow and steady ruthlessness, pumping the weapon in and out of her. The blood from my hand makes a mess, the skin fighting to heal, but the constant slide of the blade against flesh keeps the wound open. And when she moves her hips in time with my thrusts, I smile savagely against her lips.

"You are fucking perfect."

"Oh, God, Quinn, more," she begs breathlessly. "It feels so good."

"That's it," I encourage. The coppery tang of blood in the air builds a painful pressure at the base of my spine. It works its way up my rigid shaft, forcing a growl from me as I ache to bury myself inside Rapunzel. "Beg me, Princess. Beg me for what you need."

"Please…" She claws my shoulders, ripping at my flesh with her nails. "Quinn, please. I need more."

"Not good enough," I taunt.

"Your cock," she gasps. "Please. Fuck me with your cock."

"Always my obedient girl." I shift my hold on the weapon, gliding my palm over the razored blade. "Listen well, Rapunzel. I have a secret to share." With an evil grin, I rotate the sword, ripping a gasp from her. My blood, hot and thick and sticky, mixes with her slick desire to coat her drenched pussy. "A truth, if you will." Rapunzel's eyes go wide. She opens her mouth as if she's about to say something but snaps it shut. "I like when you're my good girl." Then I drive the hilt in as deep as possible without hurting her, slicing my palm to the bone. "But I love it when you're my whore."

Chapter Eleven

RAPUNZEL

"*And so it begins.*" The demon's voice drags my soul away from Quinn. The creature holds me, suspended in the darkness for what seems like forever as I grasp at nothing. Fighting for my next breath. "*The first truth has been confessed. Willingly given. By blood sealed.*"

Short.

Simple.

Not at all dramatic, as the demon sends me tumbling out of that nothingness. I land back into the moment, falling hard into the taboo pleasure of Quinn working the hilt inside me.

He pauses, his midnight eyes searching my face. "Where are you, Rapunzel?"

Where am I indeed?

"Here." I whisper my lips over Quinn's, startled at being ripped away by the demon. But also thrilled that Quinn's redemption has begun. "Right here, with you."

I shake off the encounter and allow myself to enjoy this perverse pleasure. Each controlled thrust of the steel lifts me higher. The cold can't touch me. The pebbles beneath me are nothing more than a mild annoyance. The rush of the river is soothing. I marvel at the half-moon and the stars sprinkled across the sky. Delight in Quinn's pained, panting breathing, and when I shift my lazy gaze to him…

"I love you," I rasp to the beautiful man with the midnight eyes.

The moment the revelation leaves me, I want to snatch it back and swallow it whole.

Quinn goes as still as death. The words hang suspended like a smear between us. Then he narrows his eyes and parts his lips. No words are forthcoming. I don't expect him to return the sentiment. I didn't plan on admitting this truth to him, but I was lost in the moment, and it seemed…right.

He slides the hilt out of me and tosses the sword aside. Then he kisses me with such tenderness, it overwhelms me far more than anything else he's done.

"Say it again, Rapunzel."

I cup Quinn's cheeks. "I love you."

He kisses me again. A whisper of lips over mine that comes and goes too quickly. Gently, he places my arms at my side. Blood drips like rubies from his fingertips as he starts a crimson trail down my naked flesh. Between my breasts. Along my collarbone and shoulder. His eyes, normally as dark as misery and stained with sin, are now lit with a stunning glow of…affection. Maybe even love.

Those eyes tell me what his lips can't.

Curiosity gets the better of me, and my throat catches on the gasp when I see what he's done. Quinn fingerpainted me with his blood, creating a work of art on my body that's a warped, sloppy mirror image of the markings that decorate him. As if he's baptized me with the demonic tattoos that give him his strength.

"You are…" He pauses, admiring what he's painting on my flesh. "Perfect."

I see myself through his eyes, and I feel beautiful. Adored. Loved without him having to say the words. And when he climbs on top of me, and I wrap my legs around his waist, he slides into me with a gasp.

Or was that me who made the sound?

Perhaps it was both of us.

He's watching me as he slowly rocks into me. Whispers promises in my ear of all the wicked things he'll do to me *after*. After this mess with John is over. Because what Quinn is vowing with each of those wonderfully depraved pledges is a future.

He's giving me hope.

And doing that is his way of offering me his love.

But Quinn isn't a gentle man. Nor do I need him to be anything other than who he is, and when the momentum of his thrusts builds, I bury my hands in his hair and tug. *Hard*. Hard enough to jerk his head back and rip a growl from deep within his chest. Each powerful punch of his hips scrapes my back across the dirt, and when I capture his mouth with mine, I relish his primal taste.

He understands what I'm wordlessly demanding and answers with a slam of his cock into me. My womb clenches as he sinks deep inside me that his balls slap against me. He swipes my hair away from my face and claims my mouth. Swallows my whimpers as I take his growls. And when he pulls his lips from mine, he rasps my name and fucks me so hard he scrapes me across the ground.

Each powerful, back-curling plunge sends us careening over an edge. It's like flying, weightless, with a thousand stars flashing behind my eyes. Quinn is all that's tangible, and I hold fast to him lest I float away.

"That's it, Princess," he growls. "Come for me." His demand shatters me. "Fuck. You're so goddamn pretty."

He swells inside me, and with one last hard thrust, he climaxes—and it's glorious to watch.

Quinn drops his forehead to mine. His hair curtains around us in thick, damp ropes. "Fucking say it."

I tilt my head and kiss him quickly. "I love you." Another kiss, this one on the tip of his nose. "I love you so very much, Quinn Redgrave." Resting back down, I place my palm on his back and feel the punch of his raging heart. "I love you with all of my soul."

He breathes me in. "I need…" But his sentence trails off, and he shakes his head.

Quinn isn't ready yet, and that's fine.

We have the rest of our lives for him to say it back to me.

But right now… The cold is an icy wave crashing over me when Quinn shoots to his feet. I can't don my clothes because I'm covered in blood—

"Quinn!" I'm scooped up into his arms and carried to the lake.

"You look like a human sacrifice."

That remark earns him a roll of my eyes. "I wonder who it was who painted me in his blood."

"It's the best thing I've seen you wear." His smirk is too seductive for his own good. "Unfortunately, I can't deliver you back to Wren and Dax like this."

I barely have time to gasp at the shock of icy water when Quinn leaves me in the lake to retrieve his soap bar. He returns to gently—tenderly—wash me from head to foot. My hair will take forever to dry, but I don't dare voice a single word of protest. Not even at how long he's keeping me in this frigid river. How can I complain when it feels wonderful to be cared for by this man?

When he scrubs between my legs, he grins at my wince. "If we didn't have to ride out at dawn, I'd fuck you again, right now, in this lake."

"S-some of us can a-actually feel the cold." Trembling, I remind him I'm not immune to the elements.

He gives me a peculiar look. "Who said I can't?"

"You d-don't seem c-c-old."

"Rapunzel, I'm freezing." He kisses my icy lips. "My training conditioned me to ignore the discomfort."

Discomfort? I'm on the verge of shivering to death, and he calls it discomfort.

Thankfully, Quinn cleans me quickly and, after giving himself a fast wash, carries me to the bank. He wraps me in his cloak and rubs me down to get me dry.

I'm only slightly warmer.

Quinn pulls on his clothing as well, then marches back to me. "Tonight, you gave me a gift."

Frowning, I tilt my head, my cheeks burning with a blush as I shift my gaze to the trenches we left in the dirt. "I don't know what you mean."

Quinn hooks a finger under my chin and redirects my gaze to his perfectly imperfect face. "What you said."

"Ah, that." I flick my eyes downward. "I won't take it back."

He releases my chin to tug the hood over my wet hair. "My black heart would break if you did."

For a moment, I think he's teasing. But I see the truth of his words reflected in his eyes. "I do love you, Quinn." I snake my hand from the cloak and place my palm on his damp chest. "And your heart isn't the hunk of stone you want the world to believe it is. But I'll keep that secret between us."

I've learned a thing or two about Quinn Redgrave while I've known him. He is short on words but long on actions. He gave up his soul, knowing the cost was an eternity of pain for the power to defeat a rotten king. Quinn can easily crush a man with his bare hands, yet he's gentle with me unless I need him to be rough. Despite that, he holds his strength in check, even knowing my body is indestructible. He worries for his sister. Oh, yes; he thinks we don't know, but we do. Wren, Dax, and me... We know his fear for Eleanor eats away at him and how her suffering sits at the forefront of his mind.

A man with a withered heart would have no care at all.

But he does.

He cares.

From the stories I've heard, he protects Wren and Dax in battle, taking the brunt of the damage to spare them harm.

And he loves me.

How do I know this? After we collect our belongings from the bank, he holds my hand as we walk back to the fire. Sits me on my bedroll. Has a good laugh with Wren and Dax about how long we took. Then he removes the cloak from my body and replaces it with my clothing, swatting my hands away whenever I attempt to interfere with him dressing me himself.

He even adds more wood to the fire to ensure we stay warm throughout the night.

Only once I'm duly bundled, and every tangle is brushed from my hair, does he tuck me under the blanket and take his place over by a tree at the edge of our little camp to watch over us while we sleep. He's sacrificing his rest to protect us when we're most vulnerable.

If all this isn't love, nothing is.

Chapter Twelve

DAX

Thank fucking God Lansing is intact when we arrive.

Most of it, anyway.

We can see white tendrils of smoke from the road. Those ghostly fingers reach high enough to disappear into the clouds. My stomach coils into a tight, painful knot as we charge ahead, and all I think is, *Please let her be alive*—because I'm not burying my mother. Not today. Not like this. I refuse to accept the possibility that she's dead at the hands of John's men.

Although the king's soldiers left most of Lansing untouched, they torched the village green. The merchant shops, stable, and Guildhall still smolder. They also destroyed the church, damn them. While I'm not a religious man, even I find such destruction sacrilegious.

Chaos rages around us as we race toward The Cup and Crown. As we do, I finally understand what it was like for Wren all those months ago when he rode into Leeds to find the town destroyed with a handful of royal soldiers lingering. That day, we arrived too late to save Mary Kincaid.

I fear we're too late now to save Adele Stafford.

Sweet God in heaven, if you have mercy in Your heart, please let my mother live.

The plea screams inside my mind as I take the lead, steering my horse down streets I made mischief in when I was a boy. Streets where I always felt safe, where people I've known all my life are now running in fear from men bearing the royal coat of arms. Fleeing from men I once fought beside back when I was a knight and believed John was a good man and an honorable king. But that son of a bitch made a mockery of the oath he took the day the Archbishop of Loslow placed Rygard's crown upon his head.

With my conscience abandoned on the battlefield years ago, I pull free my sword and swing my arm in a low, downward arc, slicing the first man I see draped in John's colors. I ride hard and show no mercy to the soldiers who terrorize Lancing's citizens. I slash a young soldier chasing a screaming woman, my mouth curled in a vicious grin as I send the prick to Hell where he belongs. And I keep swinging, cutting down every man wearing the red and gold of John's house that stands between us and The Cup and Crown.

As I goad my horse down the bloodied and hectic street, a glance over my shoulder shows Rapunzel and Wren directly behind me. Quinn protects our backs. The way ahead is unobstructed, and as I round the corner, I swear on all that's holy my heart freezes in my chest when I count five horses draped in John's coat of arms tied to the hitching posts outside my mother's establishment.

Goddamn it.

I hoped to arrive in time to get my mother out safely.

I hoped that for all the times my mother treated John's soldiers fairly, they would have skipped The Cup and Crown.

I hoped…

Fuck.

I hoped.

That hope dies a swift and brutal death. If even one fucking hair is out of place on her fucking head…

Instantly, rage replaces worry. And that fury is a storm that has me leaping off my horse, with each beat of my heart a painful bang inside my chest. A hand on my arm has me spinning and nearly impaling Rapunzel on my blade. "Christ—"

Rapunzel gasps and leaps back, eyes wide as she realizes how close she came to getting stabbed. "I'm sorry."

"Keep her the fuck back," I hiss.

Wren grabs her and shoves her behind me, dropping behind Quinn.

"I hear her. She's giving them hell." Quinn breaks from us and charges for the tavern. "Fuck. They know we have Rapunzel."

Rushing after Quinn, I'm vaguely aware of Wren and Rapunzel behind me. Everything is a blur. We burst inside the tavern where I grew up, and I hear—

"Where are they, Adele?" A man demands.

"Probably fucking your mother," she snaps.

"Watch your mouth, woman," the soldier warns.

His threat nonpluses my mother, who two men restrain. "You don't frighten me. I've been threatened by men twice your size and ten times your worth." She spits at his feet.

"Just because I had my hands all over your mother last night doesn't mean you can take liberties with mine. Let her go." That gets everyone's attention—even the three soldiers tearing my mother's beloved tavern apart with their mindless pillaging.

Adele whips her gaze to us. "Dax!" Then she looks back at the man standing in front of her—Captain of the Guard, judging by his finer tunic and sword—and laughs. "My son is here. You're fucked now. All of you."

"Stafford?" the Captain of the Guard smirks at me as he takes my measure. "Your filthy language seems to be your only resemblance to your mother."

Quinn steps up beside me, his menacing presence a tangible force all around us. "You'd do well to heed my friend's warning to release her."

With astounding arrogance, The Captain of the Guard moves his hand toward his sword. "Tell me, why should I listen to the words of a savage?"

A rumbling laughter works its way among the soldiers who feed off the insult of their leader.

Quinn gazes over each man in the room before settling on the bastards manhandling my mother. With a deep sigh typically reserved for toddlers who won't eat their vegetables, he responds in a monotone voice. "Because if they don't, I'll rip his arms clean out of their sockets. And that one." He jabs his index finger at the soldier on the right. "I'll use my dagger to stab him in the eyes simply because he won't stop looking at her." He gestures to Rapunzel. "Does that assuage your curiosity, or would you like to know how I plan to cut off your cock? Because men like you usually get off on roughing up defenseless women."

"Redgrave. Kincaid. Stafford." The Captain of the Guard punctuates each name by pointing at us. "Dead men, all of you, by order of King John."

"Fuck King John," Wren grinds out, then spits at the commander's feet.

In my peripheral vision, I spy the soldiers cease their plundering of The Cup and Crown to advance toward us. Quinn's growl rumbles throughout the tavern. He crouches, settles into a battle stance, and raises his sword.

"No!" Rapunzel screams, but Wren silences her with a word and pushes her back.

"Worthless, the lot of you." My mother puts up a valiant fight against her captors' hold. "Your fealty won't win you the king's favor. My son was loyal and see where it got him. John pissed all over my son's devotion to the crown," she yells in a rush. "He'll piss all over yours as well. You mark my words."

At her rant, the Captain of the Guard pauses. He gives her a peculiar look, his brows furrowed over puzzled brown eyes. Curiously, he moves his hand away from his sword. With a flick of his wrist, he gestures from me to my mother. "Quiet her, Stafford."

"Put a fucking finger on her and—"

"Dax," Rapunzel's soft voice cuts off my threat. I whip around and see her dart out of Wren's reach. Quinn, quicker than us, grabs for her, but she slaps him away. "Enough. It's time."

Not yet.

I'm not ready to let her go, and by Wren and Quinn's expressions, neither are they. But she's right. It's time, Goddamnit.

"Fucking leave her," I grind out between clenched teeth.

At that, Quinn changes his course of action and puts his body between Rapunzel and the soldiers. Everyone watches as she runs to mother and tenderly cups her face. Adele watches her curiously. Cautiously. The soldiers holding my mother's arms tense but obviously don't view Rapunzel as a threat. It's a common practice among the king's men to underestimate women.

Fucking fools.

We're counting on that to be John's downfall.

"Do you know who I am?" Rapunzel asks my mother.

"Aye, Your Highness, I certainly do. Leave it to my Dax to tangle himself up with a princess." My mother's fierce blue eyes meet calming green ones. She tilts her head and examines Rapunzel's face. "I met her once. Queen Anne. She passed through Lansing once. Not long before she fell pregnant. Her presence here was a blessing. It was as if the town had been touched by the hand of the Holy Mother Herself. This kingdom loved her, and we still mourn her loss." My mother smiles, and it's as if the rest of us cease to exist. "Your Highness, to look at you... It is to see her again. Oh, yes, I know who you are."

"Your Highness?" the Captain of the Guard echoes. "What madness is this?"

With a sneer, Wren says to him, "Look hard at her, you fucking imbecile."

The Captain of the Guard does, and when Rapunzel turns her head and the older man finally *sees* her, he issues a string of curses between clenched teeth. "Put away your weapons—"

"No, I don't think we will." Quinn's lethal laugh is devoid of genuine humor.

The Captain of the Guard heaves out a frustrated sigh. "Not you." He uses his sword to point at his soldiers. "Them. She is the lost princess, you fools."

In a profound show of respect for Rygard's princess, the man drops into a genuflect. Hand over his heart, he bows his head. The soldiers follow suit, even letting Adele go to do so. Rapunzel seizes the opportunity to pull her out of harm's way, dragging my stubborn mother to a far corner of the tavern. There, Rapunzel tucks her behind her back. Adele Stafford, however, isn't one to be treated like a feeble old woman. She nudges Rapunzel aside, spewing all sorts of insults at the king's men, with Rapunzel desperately trying to shush her.

The Captain of the Guard rises, and although he tries to rein in his soldiers, they came for a fight. John proved, yet again, how bad a king he is by recruiting the very worst of men for his army. Bloodthirsty men who, even when their captain demands they stand down, they disregard the order.

Foolish men who follow the order of a mad king always die horrific deaths.

This is a proven fact.

And when one of the men charges Wren, Quinn intercepts the attack. He moves like a lightning strike. Nothing more than a blur. While brutal, the first slash of his sword is not immediately lethal. It's a message—a warning the other men are too stupid to heed. The soldier, his right leg severed clean, gapes in shock for a moment before his wail echoes throughout The Cup and Crown. Weapon slipping from his grip, he clutches his mangled appendage. Hops once. Twice. Falls next to his limb, blood pooling around him as he gropes pathetically for his lost sword. I kick it away, laughing. Satisfaction sings through my veins as I plunge my blade into his chest.

A soldier rushes me. A sweep of my sword opens a deep gash across his midsection. Ropes of intestines spill from his belly in a wet lump at his feet. In a stupor, he peers down in disbelief at the mess. Grapples at his wound as if trying to stuff what's hanging from him back inside the gruesome cavity. He tips forward. Lands on his knees with his head bowed. His eyes rise to meet mine. Then he looks back down at his entrails on the floor. I bring my sword high, savoring the sweet rush of the moment. Gripping it in both hands, I swipe the blade down hard on the back of the man's exposed neck. One brutal slash separates his head from his body.

Movement to my right catches my attention, and I see Quinn mutilating the other soldier who restrained my mother. He tore one arm clean from the shoulder joint—as he said he would. Mounted atop the man, Quinn has his thumbs hooked into his eyes, blinding him.

"You were fucking warned," Quinn hisses.

"Enough," the Captain of the Guard yells.

No one is listening.

Wren, locked in battle with the last two soldiers, is more than holding his own—if the demented grin on his face is any indication. It's as if he's been waiting for this moment for years. I wouldn't doubt that this fight is for his mother. He still blames himself for arriving too late at Leeds to save her when John's men ravaged the village. True, he killed the soldier who murdered Mary Kincaid, but it obviously couldn't erase her death. Nor could it assuage the guilt and grief that weighs heavily on his soul.

It's almost a shame to end the beauty of the battle when the Captain of the Guard interferes and breaks up the fight.

"I said put your fucking weapons away," he snarls at the younger of the two soldiers. To the older one, "How dare you disobey my orders?"

The soldiers finally lower their weapons, with one still on the ground. "We were following the king's command."

"She is your princess." The Captain of the Guard gestures at Rapunzel. "You will obey her as you would God himself. Am I at all unclear?"

"No, Sir," they heave out, albeit reluctantly.

Rapunzel, still doing her best to shield Adele, turns to Quinn. "Will you allow my father's men to live?"

"On my soul, Princess, I'll put down my sword." The sneaky *soulless* prick falls right into the ruse.

We hadn't banked on Lansing as our battleground, with my mother caught in our plan. But if this is where it had to happen… We had just hoped for another day or two with her before we parted ways. Fuck. At least get her closer to Newkirk.

When the soldier tries to scramble to his feet, Wren gives him a nasty kick that lands him right back on his ass. My snicker draws Rapunzel and the Captain of the Guard's attention. Smirking, I shrug because who can blame me for finding humor in the bastard's pathetic bumbling as he slips and slides in his comrade's blood?

I walk backward to my mother, never turning my back on my enemy. When I reach Adele, she swats my hands away when I fuss over her to see if she's hurt. Wren coughs out a laugh at my mother's sass. I surrender, allowing her to win our little brawl. Quinn, his clothes splattered with his victim's blood, strides over to stand united with Wren.

Rapunzel, falling into her role of royal captive, sags with false relief into the captain's supportive arms. "I'm weary of all this death."

The Captain of the Guard ignores Quinn's growl, even though the chilling sound sets the hairs on the nape of my neck on end. "As am I, Your Highness." He casts a stern eye across the carnage.

And if Quinn doesn't do a better job of controlling his emotions, he's going to fuck this up because I'm reasonably sure I heard him utter under his breath, "Get your hands off of her."

Rapunzel places a hand on his arm and smiles up at him. "Are you an honorable man…?"

"Walter," he tells her. "Sir Walter Pembrook. Captain of the Guard for the royal garrison."

Rapunzel draws a somber breath. "Sir Walter, these men, my captors, are honorable as well. They have treated me well and have agreed to release me in exchange for my father's soldiers to cease the destruction of Rygard."

At Wren's confirmation, Sir Walter sneers at him. "How noble of you."

"Positively saintly," Wren drawls. "Now, do you leave without damaging the rest of Lansing, or will my friend have to slaughter the rest of your men?" He nods at Quinn. "Do we have an accord?"

Sir Walter takes Quinn's measure. "Rumor has it that you died in Haversville."

"You would do well not to believe everything you hear," Quinn growls. "And only half of what you see." He leans in close to the captain and gives him a nasty grin that is more of a sneer than a smile. Let the man get a look at his eyes and the demon's markings. "But occasionally, the stories *are* true. Best heed those."

Sir Walter, nonplused, gives him a curt nod. "Noted." Then tightly says, "In the name of King John, I accept your terms."

Quinn claps Sir Walter on the back. "Smart choice." Then he drags his gaze over Rapunzel as if he's memorizing every inch of her, just as she is right now. Her eyes wide and worried, cheeks flushed. Hands clasped in front of her. Stray strands of her golden hair worked free of the thick braid to frame her enchanting face.

By God's teeth, I'm going to miss her.

Miss her and make myself sick with worry every moment she's not in our sights.

"With that ugly business out of the way…" I sheath my sword and take Rapunzel's hand to kiss her knuckles. We lock eyes, and I wish I could freeze time and hold it in my hands forever. "Your Highness, you were a worthy opponent."

Rapunzel inclines her head. "As were you." She pulls her hand from mine and shifts her gaze to my mother. Her sad little smile breaks my fucking heart. "I'm sorry I did not arrive sooner to save more of your town."

My mother, who knows us better than anyone, gazes around Rapunzel to cast a suspicious eye at me. There is no way she believes we captured John's daughter and are simply handing her over to his men. Not with Quinn here. She must know there is more to this, and when she looks back at Rapunzel, she does it with a knowing smirk. "Your Highness, never take responsibility for someone else's behavior." She glares at Sir Walter. "Just take this scum and go."

Sir Walter guides Rapunzel to the door. Instinct must propel Wren's feet because he follows. It's Quinn who stops him by slamming an arm across his chest. A growled warning from him has Wren clenching his jaw and fisting his hands at his sides.

The remaining soldiers trail their captain and Rapunzel, their smirks galling. But it's fine. We'll remember their faces. They won't survive our invasion of Newkirk, but if they're not at the castle when we take it over, we'll eventually find them. Either way, those pricks won't live long enough to enjoy this moment of glory.

My knees weaken as I watch Rapunzel disappear from The

Cup and Crown. I want to chase after her and drag her into my arms. Protect her like I'm supposed to do.

Because I was a fucking knight.

It's what I trained for my entire life. I vowed to be honorable. To care for the innocent and the weak. Above all, to defend women.

Yet here I stand, helpless to uphold my sacred oath and safeguard the one person I love most of all.

My Rapunzel.

A glance at Quinn and Wren shows me they fight the same battle within themselves. How could they not when, from the open doorway, we see her seated on a horse? The young soldier mounts behind her. He wraps an arm around her waist, and I don't see even a sliver of sunlight between their bodies. I'm sure if it weren't for my mother's soothing touch on Quinn's shoulder, he would unleash the darkness inside him and kill these three men.

But he doesn't, and instead, covers my mother's hand with his blackened one and, without taking his gaze off of Rapunzel, says to Adele, "She was never our prisoner."

"Of course she wasn't." My mother leans closer to him and rests her head on his arm, eyes knowing. "Something tells me you three were hers."

Something tells me, as always, she's right.

And then Rapunzel is gone. Riding off toward Newkirk, and in her absence—in the space where she should be—is a void so cold and so bleak, I finally understand how it must be for Quinn not to have a soul.

"…That her?"

"The lost princess?"

"…spitting image of Queen Anne."

"But for the blonde hair."

Culbury is abuzz with whispered speculation as we ride in because, as my companion explained, rumors spread faster than a wild flame in Rygard. Word would have reached the surrounding towns that soldiers are in the area. Given who they've been searching for and that one party is traveling with a woman…

It's easy to connect to the puzzle pieces.

Not wanting to make a spectacle and add to the attention, Sir Walter insisted on keeping our traveling part small. Just him and I, and the other two soldiers from The Cup and Crown. The remaining army, he explained, follows behind us to protect our backs. I wonder if suspects my men follow as well, that they will tail us to Newkirk.

If I try hard enough, I feel them traveling stealthily back there, keeping watch over me. Their unseen presence comforts me. Helps to keep the fear away now that strangers surround me. Surrounded by the enemy.

One wrong word, one wrong *look*, will give away this game I play, one where I am the princess eager to be reunited with a father I'm excited to meet.

Draped in John's red and gold colors, I share a horse with Devan, a chatty young soldier. The tunic beneath my cloak is a garish reminder of everything I intend to steal from my father. Beside us, Roland, a stoic soldier, has done nothing but scowl at me since The Cup and Crown. He makes me uneasy.

The large and ravaged town vibrates with curiosity and an undertone of hostility. Perched atop the massive brown destrier, I flick my gaze from person to person, scanning the wary faces of those watching us as we travel along the cobblestone street. We trot by a woman who scoops her toddler up in terror. A burly man jumps in front of them. Another mom clutches her infant and races away. Most, however, stand tall. Defiant, even. Brandishing common items as makeshift weapons. I've no idea what that woman will do with her broom, but by her expression, she'd no doubt wield it with the same ferocity as a sword.

One brave man spits on the ground, his insolent gaze locked on Sir Walter. Secretly, I applaud his bravado, even as I swing my eyes to the Captain of the Guard, prepared to demand he show the man mercy should he notice the townsman's insubordination.

I tug the black hood higher over my head with a firm hand. Hunker deeper into the cloak, anxious as I enter yet another stage of this journey. We head toward the village green, surrounded by buildings in various stages of repair. Some, however, remain charred rubble. The stench of stale smoke lingers, cutting an acrid undertone on the crisp autumn air. Seeing this destruction is as heartbreaking as it is fortifying. Isolation protected me. Experiencing it for myself… Seeing the dread in people's eyes when they look at the soldiers… It reinforces my resolve. Facing my father will be my greatest challenge, but I will do it for these people. For all of Rygard.

I also do it for myself.

We'll put that bastard in the dirt where he belongs, even if I have to do the deed myself. John cannot be allowed to live. We must eliminate his evil for this kingdom to thrive.

I square my shoulders and sit straight, ignoring my companion's incessant chitchat. I ignore his arm around me as well and instead focus on the plan. Always on the plan. Have John's soldiers get me to Newkirk. Get Quinn, Wren, and Dax inside that fortress. Kill the king and take his throne.

So simple.

So very complicated.

A lovely little girl gives me a shy wave. I return the gesture, adding a gentle smile. She beams me a wide grin, revealing two missing top teeth. Adorable. Her mama snatches her hand and hauls her away, and I want to shout, 'No! Please, no! Don't be afraid. I promise your child will grow up safe.'

But I don't.

I can't.

The arm around me tightens when I shift in the saddle to adjust my weight to keep the blood flowing in my legs. "Are you well, Your Highness?"

Since Devan can't see my expression, I grimace at his question. He means well. The young soldier has been kind to me after Sir Walter ordered him to see to my comfort. He's kept up a steady conversation during the arduous hours spent sharing a saddle as we traveled across Rygard. Truth be told, though, it's been mainly one-sided, with him doing most of the talking and me doing much of the listening. If I've learned nothing else about Devan, it's that he worships my father. That makes him untrustworthy and, frankly, loathsome. Stupid as well. What a shame because with his shaggy brown hair, deep hazelnut eyes, and quick laugh, Devan is actually a friendly and handsome man. Unfortunately, his devotion to a madman spoils his few favorable qualities.

"I'm fine, Devan, thank you," I assure him. "I'll be glad to be out of this saddle if you want the truth."

We rode long past sunset yesterday, and I barely slept last night. Then we were awake before dawn and back on the road. The cold and wind and stress have me on edge.

Devan leans forward, the chainmail beneath his tunic pressing against my back. The steel, however, is cushioned by the layers of clothing that separate our bodies. "Aye, don't I know it. Sir Walter always sets a brutal pace. Good thing we'll spend the night here. I'm sure you'll appreciate a hot meal and a soft bed."

I stare straight ahead and nod. "I'd like that."

"We'll make a final, hard push for Newkirk come the morning, so get a good night's rest, Ma'am. You'll need it." Releasing me, he drapes his arm over my shoulder. Points to a cozy home at the end of the street. "See that there, the house with the tulip garden?"

"Yes, it's lovely. Why?"

"I was born in there." It's impossible to miss the wistfulness in his tone. "I lived there until I was seven, and my uncle called upon me to become his page."

Although seven seems a tender age, I've read it's normal for boys to begin training that young.

"Your uncle is a nobleman?"

"Aye, but he died a traitor's death."

I'm taken aback by the nonchalance of Devan's statement. "Did he?"

"Yes, Ma'am, he did. He was among those who dared to accuse your father of murdering King Henry."

A sensitive subject, I proceed with caution. "Yes, I've heard the accusation. I've also heard Henry was wreaking havoc throughout Rygard. Some say he was bankrupting the royal coffers and had led the kingdom into an unwinnable war against Cilicia."

"It's true, and from what my father told me, the old king slain entire families of anyone who opposed his authoritarian rule. But our good king had no part in Henry's death. 'Twas an accident."

I cannot understand how Devan can't see how John fashioned himself into a mirror image of Henry. No, that's not accurate. John is worse. Still, I say, "My father is a blessing upon this land." The lie falls hard from my tongue, but one spoken with enough conviction to persuade Devan that I believe it.

His arm wraps back around my waist in a firm but awkward hold. "You, Ma'am, are also a blessing."

"Devan, enough," Sir Walter snaps as he rides up beside us. "Your Highness, we'll bed down at The Red Bell. Of course, you'll have your own room and a bath if you'd like."

"That will be wonderful, thank you." I'm filthy and weather beaten from the cold, and privacy sounds divine. "Food and a bed are perfect."

Sir Walter, a tremendous man with a thick, blonde beard that eats up the entire lower half of his face, cuts me a sharp eye. He drags his merciless blue gaze over me, making me infinitely grateful that I'm covered from head to foot. Finally, he gives me a curt nod. "Follow me."

He goads his horse and rides ahead, with dour-faced Roland joining him. Devan spurs our horse forward. "Sir Walter may be intimidating, but he's a good man who wasn't always a curmudgeon. He's still angry that after Sir Stephan of Glasburg was murdered, he didn't immediately move up in rank as expected."

My curiosity is duly piqued. "Things failed to work out the way he planned?"

Devan's voice is low and conspiratorial. "Truth?"

I glance over my shoulder. "Of course," I whisper back.

Devan's expression is gleefully evil, that of a man who enjoys good gossip. "Ma'am, with all due respect, your father hates him."

I stash this important information away inside my mind.

"Does he? That's…surprising." I look at Sir Walter's broad back as he rounds the corner of a building. "And why is that, do you suppose?"

"Sir Walter has a strong mind, is all. He's loyal, of course, but our king… He…" Devan's sentence trails off, which stokes my curiosity from an ember to a blaze.

"Go on," I encourage him. "Speak freely, please."

He guides us around the building, trailing behind Sir Walter and Roland. The Red Bell comes into view, the quaint inn a welcome sight for sore eyes after an eternity stuck in the cradle of this man's thighs. "He was only made Captain of the Guard weeks ago, after Sir Ricard was killed when we were forced to burn Kenilworth Village."

"I see." I store this information away because Wren warned me—repeatedly—that at court, one never knows who is enemy or ally.

We arrive at The Red Bell before I can ask why they destroyed Kenilworth, but I know the answer. John's soldiers punished them for their ignorance of where I was hiding. Devan dismounts before me, then helps me off his destrier. Two strapping lads, one barely older than a child, rush from the inn. They take the reins and lead the animals away, likely to the village green, where they'll be stabled for the night.

I'm ushered inside, where I push the hood off my head and toss the braid down my back. It's been heavy, sitting on my shoulder the entire day, scratching under my chin. Now that I'm 'found,' there is no need for me to hide. The hood is strictly now for warmth.

An elderly innkeeper waits nervously in the tavern area. Her eyes downcast, she wrings her hands. The patrons likely cleared out the moment we entered Cullbury. All this open space is crowded with only a handful of polished wooden tables. The scent of roasting meat reminds me I haven't eaten a decent meal in days. There's a man, so ancient he looks more dead than alive, half-hidden in a shadowed corner. He grips a mop, watching us through one good eye. The milky one stares unseeing. His threadbare clothing hangs from his frail body.

The woman finally looks up and hope slowly creeps into her wide brown eyes as she studies me from my golden braid to the king's colors draped around my body. She extends a trembling hand. Steps toward me. "Rumors have reached us…" The breathy awe in her tone has Sir Walter waving away Devan and Roland when they move to protect me. She lowers her arm and walks backward. "Is it true? Are you Princess Rapunzel?"

"I am."

A bang drowns out the innkeeper's gasp when the mop slides from the old man's hands. She drops into a deep curtsey, and I swear the woman's nose practically touches the floor. When she finally rises, I hear the bones in her brittle knees crack. She doesn't meet my eyes. Instead, I'm left staring at the gray bun wound tightly atop her head.

"You're Highness, this is a miracle," she whispers to the floor.

I close the distance between us and grasp her visibly shaking hands. "What is your name, good woman?"

"Molly, Ma'am," she whispers, her gaze still on her feet. "Molly O'Brien."

"Although your shoes are lovely, Molly, I wish you would stop admiring them and look at me, please." I give her hands a gentle squeeze.

Molly's gaze drifts to my face. Her cheeks are bright red with a flush. "Please forgive me, Ma'am, I—"

"I'm teasing you," I tell her with a smile.

The woman, tense as a board, glances over my shoulder. Then she focuses her fretful brown eyes on me. "There were stories… Some tell of how you were held captive by a witch. Others that you were…" She grips my hands so tight my fingers crush together. The woman swallows hard, her eyes wide. "That you were dead." Her expression is full of desperation. "But many of us never believed that. I've prayed for your safe return every night. Prayed with all of my heart for your safe return."

During all those lost years in the tower, I believed myself alone. But I wasn't, was I? Rygard was with me.

"Your prayers worked, Molly. Thank you for them." As gracefully as possible, I pry my hands from hers. "I'm sorry my absence brought such pain to this kingdom."

"No, Your Highness, your return is marvelous in our eyes." The whisper of swords slipping from their sheaths sounds around us when she wraps her arms around me,

Devan and Roland jump forward again to protect me, but between me waving them back and Sir Walter's barked command for them to stand down, they lower their weapons and back away.

Molly squeezes the breath out of me. "Save us." Her rasp against my ear is so fast and low that I almost miss it. Then she shuffles away from me with her head bowed again. "When my sons return from the stable, I'll have them bring a bath to your room." Now that I've seen how young her sons are and how feeble she and the old man are, I attempt to protest. "No, Ma'am, please. Allow us the honor of extending every hospitality to you. Please, sit. I have stew brewing." She waves over the elderly man. "Uncle, make sure our esteemed guests' rooms are ready."

The white-haired man unsticks himself from the floor. Stops and bows as he passes me but refuses to acknowledge the soldiers as he ambles toward the stairs. It's an arduous trek to the second story for him, and I feel awful that he's about the task, but I hold my tongue as Molly ladles steaming stew into the bowls. Her hands are steady when she places one in front of me. I offer the kind woman my heartfelt gratitude. Those same hands shake when she presents the food to the soldiers, although Sir Walter mutters his appreciation.

Molly's panic is palpable. As if this fragile calm will shatter and erupt into violence. When her sons return, she orders them to fill a tub with hot water for me. I swear she puts them to this task solely to keep them away from the soldiers.

Out of sight, out of mind.

Out of the grave.

Although I could easily eat another bowl of stew, I refrain. I also stop myself from asking Molly about her husband, assuming he died during the raid on this town. It's as safe a guess as any.

After we finish our meal, Sir Walter escorts me to my room. Molly trails us, fussing over me to ensure I'll be comfortable for the night. She even offers me her clothing so I'll have something clean to sleep in and to wear come the morrow. I only accept her generosity because my garments are speckled with the blood of the men Quinn killed at The Cup and Crown.

Even these stains on my clothing add to the heartache of how much I miss my men. They may not be far from me, but they feel worlds away. Somehow, though, I draw on their strength to fortify mine.

Then Molly is gone, and I'm alone in this small room with Sir Walter. He takes up entirely too much space. I wish he'd leave as well.

He narrows those cunning eyes on me. "You aren't what I expected."

His statement is startling. Frowning, I cross my arms over my chest. "Am I being complimented or insulted?"

"Take it how you will."

"How I take it depends on your answer to this question. Are we enemies, Sir Walter?"

He steps forward and I stand my ground even though I want to leap back. "Is there cause for us to be enemies, Princess Rapunzel?"

With a test of the waters, I tiptoe into the tide. "Rygard has seen enough bloodshed." I unlace my arms and lift my chin. "Would you agree?"

He purses his lips and lifts a single brow. When he speaks, he does so casually, telling me a story I'm keen to learn about this man who holds the highest rank in the royal garrison. "My family is originally from Cilicia." He locks his hands behind his back and strolls to the window. 'King Henry was fond of starting pointless wars. One of those was against my homeland. He picked a fight with Queen Zara, claiming she shamed him by rejecting his marriage proposal. Of course the offer was a sham. The queen would never accept a foreign husband. Cilicia's royal family are notorious for marrying their own."

"But that's… That's repugnant." As much as I try, I can't keep the shock—and revulsion—from my voice.

"In this, we agree. Their inbreeding may keep the bloodline pure. But." He taps his temple. "It broke their minds. They rule with an iron fist. Their tyranny makes life in Cilicia a living hell. When presented with a choice of evils, my father believed Rygard was the lesser of the two. At least there was the hope that Henry's son would be this kingdom's salvation." He stops and turns to me. "Although grown when my father snuck us across the border into Rygard, for me, it was…a homecoming. A paradise after Henry was killed. At least for a while." His mouth lifts in a hint of a sardonic grin as he advances on me, one slow and steady step at a time. "Now that you've spent time with Kincaid, tell me, Princess, is it true? Did Percy murder Henry so John could take the throne?"

This time, I retreat and keep going until I collide with something solid, and I can't back up farther. Caught between two unyielding objects, Sir Walter and the wall, I drag in a fortifying breath and lick dry lips. "Why would I know?"

The question tumbles like the flakes of a brittle, crumbled leaf from my mouth.

Percy *did* dispatch the arrow that struck Henry in the eye, and he did it at his dearest friend John's request.

"Why, indeed?" Sir Walter studies me for a long moment. As if he could pry the answers to questions asked and unasked. "A word of wisdom, if you will. In this kingdom, under this king's rule, secrets have a far greater cost than a person is willing to pay. If you want your head to remain on your shoulders, you will do well to keep your secrets close to your heart." Then he leans low and says in a harsh whisper. "Know this, Princess Rapunzel. I pledged my allegiance to Rygard. My loyalty is to this kingdom. My sword belongs to these people. I have never used it against a loyal Rygradian." He pulls back. "Devan and Elric won't be joining us on the morrow."

Shaken, puzzled, I watch him stalk from the room. I put a hand to my mouth to stifle a sharp exhale of breath. My legs give way from the impact of his confession. I slide to the floor, not knowing how long I sit there, legs drawn to my chest, arms wrapped around my thighs, with Sir Walter's words echoing in my mind on repeat.

He's not a man I want as my enemy.

But he isn't my enemy, is he?

I have to grip the edge of the linen-covered straw mattress for balance as I regain my feet. Sir Walter didn't threaten me. He told me, without actually telling me, that he is not loyal to John. As he said, he's loyal to *Rygard*. There is a difference. A *vast* difference. I don't dare reveal our plans. Not yet. Only when I know for certain I can trust him.

With a bit more optimism than I had when this day started, I strip off my sullied clothing and take advantage of the tepid bathwater. Unfortunately, the loneliness returns after I finish with a quick wash to clean away the road dust. My thoughts run to Wren, Dax, and Quinn. This room is too dark, even with the gentle glow of the fire flickering in the hearth. It's too quiet. Too…empty…without them.

Soon, we'll be reunited. When we are, we'll rebuild and bring peace to this kingdom that will last a lifetime.

Chapter Fourteen

DAX

"Ever have a moment where you think, 'Oh, God, I fucked up?'" Wren strolls out from behind a tree, arrow notched and aimed at the heart of the soldier I caught skulking around our camp. He's one of the bastards who escorted Rapunzel from The Cup and Crown, who we've been following since Lansing. "Consider this your moment."

"Go to hell," he hisses.

"Feisty. I like it. Unfortunately, you bore me with your unoriginal response." Standing behind him with my arm banded around his chest and my dagger at his throat, I have him trapped in my hold.

"Truly. Why can't people curse us to a tavern?" Wren drifts closer with a roll of his eyes. Never, though, does his arrow waver from its intended target. "Now, how about you tell us why you're following us? Otherwise, I'll have my friend here." He motions to Quinn, leaning against a tree, looking deceptively disinterested in this situation. "Pluck an eyeball from your socket and have you watch with the other while he crushes it beneath his boot. He had such a good time blinding your friend that he might want another go at it."

The middle-aged man, with his pinched-up face, presses his back against my chest in a pathetic attempt to distance himself from Wren's graphic threat.

"Fantastic," I say, laughing. Because I'm an instigator, I nudge the man forward. "Never too soon for another eye gouging."

"You're insane," Sour-Face breathes. "The lot of you."

"That's a bit of a step up from '*go to hell*.'" I press the blade deeper into his neck, and he sucks in a sharp breath between his clenched teeth. "But still banal because now you're simply acknowledging the obvious. Be a good boy, won't you, and tell us why you're nosing around where you don't belong?"

"I won't tell you a damn thing."

I blow out an exaggerated sigh. I give him a nasty nick on the side of his throat for his tenacity. "Why do they always have to be so goddamned difficult?"

"Because they foolishly believe wearing the king's colors makes them invincible," Quinn grits out, still not looking up from his mundane task of cleaning his nails. Of course, with his vision, he sees fine through the dim moonlight.

Wren steps closer, his bow gripped tight and leveled at our captive's heart. Not that he'd shoot. If he did, the arrow's force would go straight through the man's body and into mine. Hopefully, this twit doesn't realize this.

"One way or the other, you *will* tell us what we want to know," Wren assures him with a sneer. "It's just a question of how long it will take us to break you."

"Here's a hint," I taunt him. "It never takes long, but it gets bloody."

With a subtle twist of his head, the man shifts his gaze to Quinn. "Fuck you."

I give him a slight jostle. The blade skids along his flesh, cutting deeper. "That's the spirit. You're going to let us play. How fun." Then I give a little shrug that has Wren lifting a brow at me in exasperation. He takes himself much too seriously. "For us, anyway. Not so much for you."

"Go on then," he snarls. "You think I'm scared of that one because he drinks the blood of babies? Let him rip out my heart. I don't give a shit." He hocks a mouthful of spit at Quinn. "I'm the king's man. A God-fearing man. And him… He's a heathen."

Before he's even finished, Quinn shakes his head and shoves away from the tree. Wren keeps the arrow notched but lowers the bow. Quinn strolls toward us. I unwrap my arm from around the man's waist and remove the dagger from his throat. Then I lift my leg to kick him in his ass. He stumbles to the ground at Quinn's feet. "I drink the blood of babies? No," Quinn drawls. "Rip out the hearts of men? That one is true. It's not God you need to fear right now. It's me."

"Your eyes…" he breathes.

"That's right. They have the devil in them,' I say with ominous delight.

Quinn throws a deadpan look at me. "Demon."

"Demon. Devil. Same difference," I counter.

"Someone is getting shot with this fucking arrow if he doesn't start talking." Wren snarls.

Quinn grabs the man by the shoulders and drags him a few feet to slam him against the nearest tree. The man huffs as the wind gets knocked out of him. He turns away and squeezes his eyes shut when Quinn bares his teeth in a growl that reverberates throughout the quiet thicket of the trees of our camp.

"Did Sir Walter send you out here?" Quinn demands.

"Yes," he grits out, his jaw clenched.

"Why?" Wren asks.

The man glances at Wren but snaps his gaze back to Quinn, who is the more significant threat here. "On his order, you're to be killed."

Quinn grunts out a laugh.

"He can't be that stupid," Wren remarks.

"He's not," Quinn snaps and slams the soldier against the tree again.

"I'm just following orders," the soldier grunts.

Smirking, I fling the dagger straight up, spinning it. I catch it by the hilt. A trick I perfected while a member of the royal garrison long before this fool joined the ranks. Back when serving our king had honor attached to it. "As sheep do."

"You obeyed the orders of a fucking imbecile," Quinn growls. "And for that, you're going to die." With a flick of his head, he motions to an area to his left. "Don't put away your bow, Wren. There's one more hiding in the trees. I can smell him. He pissed himself. Do you want me to handle this piece of shit, or do you want me to go kill the other one?"

"This one is ours." I tap the blade against my palm, eager to get a kill in. "Go do your primal hunt and torture thing with the other one."

Quinn's grin sends a goddamn chill right down my spine. For a moment, I almost pity his prey. Almost, but not quite. Fuck these soldiers. And fuck this one's sudden weeping.

Apparently, he is plenty afraid.

Look at him, a grown man crying. A royal soldier sobbing with snot running from his nose.

He certainly was brave moments ago when he spits at Quinn's feet.

Where's his bravado now?

"Come on now." With one hand, I grab him by the collar of his tunic. "At least die like a man."

He locks his limbs. "I have a family."

Did this lice-infested pig testicle mention family to *me*? The audacity.

I shake him with such force, I'm shocked I don't snap his fucking neck. "As do I, and yet you had no problem walking into The Cup and Crown intending to kill my mother, you piece of shit."

"I'm sorry."

"They always are," Wren says with a nasty laugh. "After the fact."

Up comes the dagger still gripped in my hand as the not-so-distant screams of a man being slaughtered cuts across the night. "We're going to enjoy hurting you for taking the wrong side in this war between King John and the people of Rygard."

As a second scream reaches us, Wren drops his bow to switch to his sword—and while we don't waste too much time on him, we do make damn sure he learns the meaning of the fucking word 'sorry' by the time we're finished with him.

Chapter Fifteen

JOHN

I am not an easily flustered man, but I am awestruck as I watch the woman enter my hall.

My God, Rapunzel is Anne reborn.

Of course, I must look past her hair—that glorious, golden hair—to see the resemblance, but it's there. With each step she takes toward me, the hand of grief tightens its hold around my heart. It's a reminder of the day when my Anne told me she was with child. That day, I was a man elated. But it was a joy that ended the day this woman took Anne from me.

This woman, Rapunzel, owes me a debt.

A life for a life.

I sit proudly on the throne, crowned head high and jaw set. I want her to see me. Behold the king who burned his kingdom to find her. That is the power I wield. Yet, this slip of a woman— my daughter—refuses to lift her eyes. She stares at the ground as she marches through the crowd of curious courtiers. Her false display of docility does not trick me. Any dolt can see the strained majesty in her graceful movements. The room crackles with the force of her courage. No, I am not fooled by her façade of timidity.

Not at all.

Nothing can break a noble spirit, not even a lifetime in a tower.

Finally, she and Sir Walter reach the dais. She lifts her head. Her eyes meet mine, and Anne is again in the large emeralds that pierce through me. Those eyes see beyond my crown and throne and fine garb. They behold the grief that chaffs me raw whenever I think about my wife. And even deeper still. To the sickness slowly rotting me to death.

Before I address her, I first give my attention to Sir Walter. Let her wait. It's an act of power, this, to put her in her place. Also, to allow me to compose myself before speaking directly to her. Blast the woman for having this irksome…unnerving… effect on me.

I may not like the man, but Sir Walter is steadfast in his devotion to Rygard, so I say, "You have the crown's appreciation for delivering the lost princess to us."

Sir Walter inclines his head. "It is my greatest honor to reunite her with Your Majesty."

"I trust we did not lose many good men during this endeavor?"

"Regrettably, we did, Sire."

"Terrible shame," I say with a somber *tsk,* as if I care about the loss of a handful of soldiers. Anyone and everyone were expendable against the need to get Rapunzel safely to me. And when I finally angle toward her and extend my hands, she takes them, and I note how she trembles. Good. She should be frightened. "Welcome home, Daughter. I have waited for this moment since the day you were stolen from me."

"As have I, Your Majesty," she whispers.

"You are not what I expected," I admit to this stranger staring at me through Anne's eyes.

Her small, shy smile is, I hate to admit, captivating. "Nor are you."

I drop her hands and clasp mine behind my back and puff out my chest. The action causes a rumble in my lungs, forcing me to fight a cough. I will not appear weak. Not when this woman, who, despite her quiet voice, brazenly meets my stare. She does not cower before me. Impressive, yes, but also grossly insolent. Remarkable how she stands there, bold as you please with that hair. That fucking hair infused with Sybil's magic—and tainted with my wife's death. It falls to her knees in golden waves, mocking me. Remind me how each day I can't use its magic is one more day this sickness inside me inches me toward my grave.

If I wasn't aware of the consequences, I'd have my guards hold her down while I cut every strand off her head.

And yet, I admire the regal lift of her chin and the determined set of her shoulders. The more I study her, the more I reluctantly admire much of myself in this striking stranger. My Anne was a gentle woman, may her soul be at peace. Perfect in all ways. She knew her place, unlike this woman, who…

Who was spared the rod and allowed to retain the arrogance she inherited from me.

"What did you expect, my dear daughter?"

"A monster," comes her quick reply. Then with an embarrassed laugh, adds, "Complete with horns."

I must pretend I am a pleased father finally reunited with his daughter. I let out a hearty laugh and tap the points of the gold crown atop my brown curls. "No horns here."

Rapunzel moves closer to Sir Walter and tilts her head to regard me through narrowed eyes. "And yet you destroyed half your kingdom and slaughtered innocent people to find me. I'm curious, Father. Are those not the deeds of a monster?"

A glance over her head shows the courtiers listening intently to our conversation. I should have dismissed them when the guards alerted me she had arrived. Damn my arrogance in thinking she would have come in cowed. How dare this woman be so arrogant? How *dare* she question me? Why doesn't she fear me? If I so choose, I could toss her in my dungeon alongside Sybil. Take her hair instead of choosing to bide my time and ask it from her. *It is my fucking right as king.*

As her father.

But because a piece of Anne lives inside this woman, I choose to be benevolent toward her and extend a kindness I would never show another living soul.

"No, Rapunzel." I draw on patience that will quickly wear thin should be press me. "They were the actions of a desperate father." I step off the dais, keenly aware that every eye is on us. Of Sir Walter looming, primed, and tracking me as I wrap my arms around my daughter. "We are together now. Our family can heal. My only regret is that your mother is not here to celebrate this glorious day with us."

Rapunzel's arms hesitantly snake around me, and a cheer erupts throughout the hall. The noise almost drowns out her whispered question that sounds too close to my ear.

"We are not enemies?"

Perhaps. Perhaps not.

"That, Daughter," I say low enough for only her to hear. "Remains to be seen."

She pulls out of my embrace but doesn't step away. "May I speak plainly, Your Majesty?"

I give her the slightest incline of my head, displeased at my curiosity about what she might say. "Of course."

"I have lived the whole of my life as a prisoner. First Sybil's, then Wren Kincaid's. All I ask for is freedom. My loyalty lies with the person who grants me the liberation I crave. No, that's wrong." Tears wet her incandescent eyes. "The freedom I *deserve.* So, I ask you, King John of Rygard, are you my father or my captor?"

Dare I believe the sincerity behind her words? I would have Rapunzel compliant in my plan to use her hair to cure my illness.

Although I've committed a trove of sins that will land me in Hell, I'm not willing to add Anne's heartbreak to the pile. Forcing our daughter's compliance will tear my beloved's soul apart. If I face Anne in the afterlife, how can I tell her I harmed her child?

Unless Rapunzel proves too stubborn and leaves me no choice.

"I am your father, Rapunzel."

Her relief is palpable. "I'm glad. I've been so lonely." She closes her eyes a moment, the tears finally breaking to cut a path down her smooth cheeks. "I would… I would love you if you let me."

My dubious nature warns me not to trust her. But Anne. She looks so much like Anne… No, Rapunzel's face must not deceive me. My daughter will have the illusion of freedom while being my prisoner. And as for love, that she can keep. What need have I of such a useless emotion when whatever love that lived inside me died with my wife?

Chapter Sixteen

RAPUNZEL

The memories of the tower move through my mind like fragmented dreams. Broken images that somehow no longer find a proper fit when pieced together. And yet, the desolation that marks my soul from my time there is a part of me. A skin I wear beneath the one the world sees. It was easy to forget how it stretched and moved and wrapped itself around me when I was at Dyhurst. There, I was happy. I was…loved. Here, suspicious eyes watch me.

Here, nowhere here is safe.

I've been at Newkirk for a sennight. The time has crawled over me like a march of insects across my flesh. The more I pretend that Wren and Dax and Quinn were merely my benevolent captors who released me to face Lansing, the further I feel from them. I haven't dared to whisper their names aloud for fear these walls have ears. Instead, I chant them inside the privacy of my mind during the lonely, endless nights.

I've yet to meet Eleanor. Nor had John allowed me to see Sybil. Wisely, I've not pressed to see either woman lest I rouse his suspicions about further—or rile his temper. Eleanor spends most of her time hiding in her room. Hiding from her husband.

He refused her the Queen's Chamber. My mother's room lay empty and perfectly preserved until I arrived. John couldn't bring himself to have another woman invade her space—until I showed up on his doorstep, and he put me in there.

Life at Newkirk is my version of the wrong side of the afterlife because being here is akin to Hell. Presided over by an imposter devil with a false benevolent smile and an obnoxious laugh.

A guard follows me everywhere. Suspicious eyes track me. Curious stares study me. Since I entered this fortress, I've been a prisoner disguised as a princess. But above all, John's distrust, his illusion of civility—is a noose wrapped around my neck. One that tightens the longer I must wait for the perfect moment to put the final stage of our plan into action.

As I stride toward the monster I'm forced to call Father,

John's icy grin pulls me forward. One foot in front of the other. Whispers sound around me from the shrewd but needy courtiers who crowd this gilded hall. All vie for the attention of Rygard's found princess. They are background noise. Silly creatures easily ignored.

I have crossed paths with Sir Walter, though. He says nothing to me, but his eyes always seem to see too much. Seem to see those secrets he warned me to keep close to my heart.

"There she is," John announces with a dramatic clap. However, the sparkle in his eye when he spies my blonde waves is genuine. Last evening over dinner, I caught him attempting to touch it, and I nearly gagged on my roasted pork. I had to wash down the bile with a hearty swallow of spiced wine lest I disgrace myself at the king's table in front of a roomful of nobles. "Rapunzel, that blue on you. You are your mother reborn."

I'm wearing a lovely sapphire frock decorated with intricate gold embroidery. Suddenly, I wonder if I'm wearing *her* gown. It wouldn't be beyond John to dress me in my mother's clothes. In many ways, he's trying to recreate her by putting me in her room, presenting me with her jewels, and constantly reminding me of how my temperament is akin to hers.

I wonder if this is for my benefit, to connect me to a mother I never met—or to keep him from killing me by constantly reminding himself that I am a product of his beloved wife.

"Thank you." I force up the corners of my mouth in a false grin. When I reach the dais, I snag a bit of the velvet, gold-edged skirt and give it a gentle swish. "Although I appreciate these gifts, I must insist you stop. You're spoiling me."

Yesterday, he presented me with a beautiful brown mare he'll never allow me to ride.

These gifts may be grand, but they are empty. A display for the nobles who peck at his feet like chickens seeking crumbs. To show them how much he loves me by showering me with frippery.

John slowly rises. I note his slight sway. He touches the arm of the throne and holds still for the briefest of moments. "And what else am I to do with my fortune other than spend it on my daughter?"

Use it to better the lives of your people.

Of course, I swallow the retort and step onto the dais to accept his outstretched hand. He pulls me into his arms, and it's an effort not to recoil from his embrace. His touch makes my skin crawl. Worse, he rests his cheek against the side of my head and buries his hand in my hair as if he's cradling me. "I trust you are well?"

"I am, thank you." I allow this farce of affection to go on for as long as possible, then push away. "You've made me very welcome in your home."

Lies. I am a captive, and I want to see Sybil and Eleanor.

"My home?" John *tsks* at me with a playful wag of his finger. "Our home." Then he turns to regard his courtiers. To me, they are a nest of vipers lying in wait to strike. "It's been eight glorious days since our lost princess has returned to us, and while we've rejoiced in our reunion, our queen has yet to celebrate this good fortune with us. But a new day has dawned." He looks beyond the gathering of people to the opening chamber door that reveals a tiny, feminine version of Quinn.

Eleanor, quite simply, is exquisite.

Her bold red and gold gown is striking against her fair skin and plaited-to-perfection raven hair. Her steps are measured and graceful as the crowd parts for her. The only sound heard is the rustle of fabric as the courtiers curtsey when she strides past them. Her eyes are downcast, their color a secret. She steps onto the dais and slides her tiny hand into John's. Her wedding band is an ugly reminder that she's as much a prisoner here as I am.

"Good day, *Wife*." John stresses the last word right before placing a kiss on her cheek. Thankfully, he doesn't notice Eleanor's barely perceptible wince. John, a handsome man twice her age, has an evil heart and rotten soul that makes him ugly. I can't imagine she enjoys his touch, and as he inspects his young wife from head to foot, she compresses her lips and raises her eyes to the ceiling. She won't find it there if she's seeking a momentary refuge from his unwanted attention. "You look lovely on this fine morning."

"Thank you, Your Majesty," she murmurs, redirecting her gaze back at John. "As always, you were correct. Rest was all I needed." I hadn't realized I'd been waiting to hear her voice with bated breath until she spoke. When she turns to me and pins me with her mesmerizing sapphire eyes, the air leaves my lungs in a whoosh. "It's a pleasure to finally meet you, Princess Rapunzel."

I never asked Quinn the color of his eyes before he lost his soul, and they turned black. Now, however, I wonder if they were as rich a blue as his sister's. Wonder if his cheeks held the same slight flush. Thinking of him brings thoughts of Wren and Dax, and an ache takes hold of me so strong I blink back tears lest they spill and give away my pain.

I drop into a curtsey. "The pleasure is mine, Your Majesty."

She doesn't allow me to stay on bended knee. Eleanor helps me straighten, and when she does, there's a tremble in her touch. "I've been eager for your return."

"That she has," John says, interrupting our conversation. "Word reached us at court that her brother was among the men who held you captive. Tell us, Rapunzel, what they say about Quinn Redgrave. Is it true? Is the man damned or not?" The king speaks loudly, theatrically. For the benefit of the crowd. Heedless of his wife's grimace caused by his callous question.

John knows.

Of course he knows. The king sent his soldier out with a blade tainted with Sybil's poison because he knew it was a sure way to defeat Quinn. Also, wouldn't Sir Walter have told him after what happened at The Cup and Crown? Unless he hasn't—because he's loyal to Rygard, not John.

Keep your secrets close to your heart…

Eleanor's distress is killing me. I wish I could give her a word—a look—to let her know Quinn lies in wait beyond the walls. Ready to strike.

Ready to free Rygard.

To save her from John.

"It's as you said. I was Wren's captive. For my protection, he limited contact with anyone besides him. But yes, I recall something odd about Redgrave." I can't say his given name. It's too… personal. I'm afraid he'll hear something in how I say it that will give away the game.

John has trod carefully when we've discussed my life in the tower and what came after. We do this dance where he tosses out the occasional question and I answer with lies laced with a light peppering of truth. Beneath our fragile civil discourse, we both know the other is deceitful. It's a deranged tug and pull wherein we wait to see who will break first.

This madman forgets that twenty-four years spent in a tower ingrained in me tolerance and fortitude he can't comprehend.

I'll never yield.

A man with his temper and character can't suppress his true nature.

He'll break first.

"Odd, you say? Interesting." If he thinks I'll wither under the weight of his glare, he's mistaken. After many long, tense moments, he claps his hands again and turns to Eleanor. "You'll stop this foolishness about your brother. It grows tiresome."

Eleanor vigorously blinks back tears. She swallows hard and slaps a false grin on her face. "I apologize, my king. No more."

I can only imagine what her 'foolishness' must be. Hoping for news that he's alive? Perhaps she's begged her husband to show her brother mercy.

John waves a hand through the air, doing a terrible job of hiding his irritation. "My wife has a tender heart, especially for her treasonous brother. One day soon, you and I will have a conversation about Wren Kincaid and his band of bastards, Rapunzel, and I expect you to tell me what you know." There's a blatant threat in his tone. He doesn't look at me when he says this. Rather, he proceeds to his dais, back on his throne without tearing his gaze from his courtiers. "Play us a carole!"

The musicians huddled in the corner begin their song, and it's like John issued an unspoken order to the nobles who fall in step to dance. How sad, how utterly pathetic they are. They glance at the king, vying for his attention. Seeking praise like dogs begging their abusive master for love.

Eleanor takes her seat on a smaller throne on John's right. I sit on the one to his left. He brought it in for me the day after I arrived when he formally presented me to his court as Rygard's lost princess.

As this kingdom's heir.

"Rapunzel, do you dance?"

At Eleanor's question, I peer around John at the gorgeous woman who resembles my Quinn. "Unfortunately, no," I say over the spirited music. "There was a sad lack of dancing partners in my tower."

My reply makes her laugh, but John ruins it by giving my shoulder a little shove. "Well, there will be plenty of dancing here. Isn't that so, Eleanor?"

Eleanor will slip through the cracks between the stones if she makes herself any smaller. "Yes, John. Your court is always lively."

"Bah," he huffs, slapping his hands on his thighs in frustration. "As if you would know." He pins me with his sharp brown eyes. "Young though she is, my wife has a weak constitution. She's always hiding in her chamber complaining of mysterious ailments" He doesn't even spare Eleanor a glance, instead watches the dancers when he sneers, "Can't even give me a child. What good is she?"

My first inclination is to sympathize with Eleanor for being unable to bear children, but I spy her subtle relief. It brings Emma's words curious remark back to me.

Some women are barren by choice.

Of course, I hadn't known what my friend meant by that statement.

I understand now.

Rygard's queen may appear docile, but she is a Redgrave. She is a survivor. And when she slides her gaze back to me, I send her a knowing little grin and the faintest incline of my head. She answers back with a wink, and although we didn't say a word, we had an entire conversation.

She just became my greatest ally.

"**D**id my brother truly hold you captive?"

Startled by the whisper, I blink against the glare of the midday sun. My hand stills on the flower's stem I'm about to pluck. I shield my eyes with the other and peek between dirty fingers to see Eleanor standing over me. My breath catches when I glance around the garden and realize we're as alone as we can be. Our guards linger a few yards away, as do her five vexing ladies-in-waiting. John appointed those arrogant noble women to follow his young wife wherever.

No doubt they report back to him.

Despite the cold, I needed a reprieve from the keep's oppressive gloom and the constant babbling of the courtiers. And thank goodness I did. We might not have had this precious—and fleeting—somewhat private moment if I hadn't.

"No, Eleanor, he did not," I answer so softly the words are nearly lost on the breeze.

"I never believed that nonsense." Eleanor nervously chews on her bottom lip. Her eyes remind me of the violent waters of the Lennox Sea. "Is he…? I miss him, Rapunzel."

"He misses you as well." It takes everything I have not to

wrap this tiny woman in my arms and share in her misery. "And he loves you very much."

Her scheming ladies and our guards trail us. Behind them is Eleanor's guard, with mine taking the rear as we stroll Newkirk's eastern garden.

With an exaggerated huff, Eleanor stops walking and spins to glare at the harpies behind us. In a show of frustration, she tosses her hands in the air. "This is absurd. I require a moment of peace. Rapunzel and I are walking the garden, not headed into battle. Shoo, all of you. You," she motions to the ladies. "Go gather fresh flowers for the hall and you," she gestures to our guards. "I can hardly hear myself think, much less carry on a conversation with all the stomping behind us. You couldn't sneak up on a sleeping infant making all that noise. Keep back so I may have a proper chat with Rapunzel and acquaint myself with our lovely lost princess." Then to me, in a murmur, "That she should get them to leave us alone for a bit."

My jaw hangs agape, and I have to snap it closed. "Bravo, Your Highness," I murmur.

"I'm not as docile as I make them believe," she whispers.

No, she's certainly not.

After all, Eleanor is a Redgrave. After getting to know one very well, I can confidently say they have fire in their blood.

The ladies don't have to be told twice. They scurry off to do their queen's bidding. As for the guards, well, they step back a few paces, but they do it reluctantly. But at least they do it, leaving us to speak more privately.

Eleanor's lashes glisten with unshed tears. "Walk with me, Rapunzel."

She links her arm with mine and keeps her voice low enough that her words cannot drift to the listening ears behind us. "Please tell me, as no one else here speaks to me. Did he do that blasphemous thing they claim?"

I want to lie to her. Lord knows I do, but time works against us, leaving no room to pad the truth. "He gave up his soul for the strength and speed to kill John." She takes a moment to absorb this, but with a stern nod, she squares her shoulders and pulls her composure around herself like a shield. "But there's hope for him. I can't tell you how I know this, but you must trust me. Please, trust me. Can you do that?"

"When we were children, I was always getting myself into mischief. Quinn saved me every time." She tilts her head to close her eyes and lets the midday sun bathe her face. "I suppose this is his way of saving me now." She lowers her chin and opens her eyes. She stares straight ahead, anguished as if watching a terrible scene play out only she sees. "He killed our father. The day Stephan came to take me away to court. Quinn tried to stop him, but Stephan was the superior swordsman back then. It didn't help that our father interfered. He sided with Stephan, of course, and when Quinn had his back to him, our father... He stuck him with a blade. What father does that, Rapunzel?" *Mine*, but I keep that thought tucked inside my mind. "In the end, Quinn's fight was for naught. As Stephan dragged me out, literally kicking and screaming, the last thing I saw was Quinn slitting our father's throat. The rumors began about him losing his soul soon after." Her eyes glisten with raw guilt, which cuts me to the quick. "It's my fault. All of this."

"No, Eleanor, that's not true," I rasp. "It's John's fault. Stephan's fault. Your father's fault." Oh, God, Quinn killed his father. That must fester on his conscience. "Everything Quinn did, he did because he loves you. Because he believed it was the right thing to do. All that he does now is for you. For us. For Rygard."

Eleanor watches me through her tears, her perceptive gaze searching. "You love him."

No need to deny it. "I do. I love him, Eleanor, and I will do everything I can to keep him alive."

And help him get his soul back.

Eleanor wipes the stray tears that slip down her reddened cheeks and recomposes herself. She reminds me of a perfect flower petal. Fragile, yet able to withstand a storm. "I didn't want to believe you'd be loyal to *him*."

Him, of course, being John.

"That man will not be king for much longer. I swear this to you."

She seems to contemplate this for a moment, chewing her lip before saying, "John keeps Sybil in the dungeon. She's hurt, but I don't know the extent of her injuries. Only that he's taken her ability to weave spells."

That news is a punch to my gut. The garden spins, and I'm dangerously close to emptying my stomach of the fruit and bread I ate for breakfast.

Dear God…

John must have taken her tongue. It's the only way to rob her of her craft. Without a tongue, she can't speak her spells. No one else can say the words in her stead. Only she must voice them. That's the nature of magic. If anyone could wield it…anyone could wield it. One must be born with the ability to bend reality using the powerful combination of potions and words.

A witch who cannot speak is no witch at all.

"Help me, Eleanor," I beseech her in a rough whisper. "Please, help me. Your brother lies in wait just outside of Newkirk. Help me get him inside the castle so we can kill John."

"Yes." She's already nodding. "Of course, I'll help you," she rasps. "We can do this, and we won't be alone. Others here will fight with us, but it will be dangerous."

"I'm prepared for dangerous," I assure her. "What I'm not prepared to do is let that madman continue to terrorize Rygard."

"Good, I'm glad" Her smile is sweet, and there's a sparkle in her blue eyes. "Now, tell me, Rapunzel, how did you come to love my brother?"

I pick my words carefully, keeping Emma's warning about

how others will take my relationship with my men at the forefront. Rather, I feed her bits and pieces of how Quinn bartered his soul and how he, Wren, and Dax came to be as close as brothers. I tell her of Dyhurst, Emma, and the renegades who call that ancient castle home. Then I explain how there's a chance Quinn can gain his soul back, leaving out the details, lest I say too much and break my pact with the demon. Last, I tell her of the awful day we came too close to losing Quinn when his throat was slashed with a poisoned blade.

And when I'm done, I find her gaping at me.

No, that's not right.

She's staring at my hair.

Instinctively, a hand flies to the heavy braid. I wince when I realize how much I've said. *What* I've said. I added one detail without thinking because the words flowed once I began talking.

"You healed my mortally wounded brother with your *hair*?"

I roll my lips between my teeth and nod because it's too late to take back the truth. I spent my life guarding this secret. But after ten minutes with Eleanor, it flowed out of me like a rushing river. I blame it on the fact that she looks too much like Quinn.

With nothing more to hide about my hair, I explain how John called for Sybil to heal my mother after she fell ill while she was pregnant with me. How Sybil's magic couldn't save Queen Anne, and instead, infused me with life. How the magic seeped into my hair, and because of that, I can heal the sick and the dying.

I even confess that my life is connected to the magic.

She asks questions, many of which I answer. Some I can't because I don't understand how the magic works. I only know it does. We walk a bit more, and finally, the conversation turns, and she tells me of the Redgraves. How they were proud and powerful before their father's greed destroyed their family. She was betrothed to Sir Stephan of Glasburg since she was a child. Although never pleased with this match, she was prepared to do her duty and marry him. But after Queen Anne's death, an opportunity presented itself. John needed a new wife, and she was offered up like a sacrificial lamb to a king mad with grief.

The king gained a pretty young bride to abuse.

Glasburg rose in rank to become Captain of the Guard.

Quinn murdered his father before the man could reap the benefits of the power promised to him. Then he surrendered his soul and tore out Glasburg's heart with his bare hand.

Two down…one left to kill.

Chapter Eighteen

RAPUNZEL

"*Wake up.*"

A haunting voice slithers into my dream, but it evaporates like smoke.

Sybil? No. Hers reminds me of two stones grating against each other.

Tucked into my warm bed, I roll over and tug the heavy blanket with me. I keep my eyes shut tight, knowing when I open them, the floral murals I painted across the plaster walls of my tower will surround me. An artist I'm not, but I had to pass the endless days somehow. When I ran out of parchment, I used my prison as a canvas, bringing to life the outside world as I imagined it.

I swore to Sybil that I would never leave the tower, and I never did, even allowing her to shackle me to my cage lest I give in to the temptation of freedom.

Not even after discovering where she'd hidden a master key that would grant me liberation did I dare step one foot outside. Fear, I found, was a stronger chain…

…until Wren seized me from my tower and introduced me to a world of possibilities.

"Rapunzel, please. You must wake up."

It's the urgency in the voice has me bolting upright in bed. Disoriented, I frown into the darkness.

I gather the linen blanket to my bosom. Swivel left and right, scanning the darkened room. All the air leaves my lungs when I spy a shadowy figure that seems birthed from the darkness. It moves toward the bed, pressing me back against the pillow.

Not the demon. It's much too small…

"Eleanor!" I rasp, keeping my voice low so the night guard outside my chamber won't hear me. "How did you get in here?" I whip a petrified glance at the door. "If anyone catches you—"

The smoldering ash in the hearth casts barely any light. However, I vaguely see her extend a slender arm as she points to an open secret wall panel across the room. "The Queen's Passage," she whispers. "We have little time. I spoke to Sir Walter. He will help us. Hush, Rapunzel," she scolds when I attempt to speak. "I trust him and ask that you trust him as well. §He'll find Quinn and tell him where to enter the keep." She grabs my hands, forcing me to drop the blanket. "We won't fight John alone. Walter said there are men in the garrison who despise John. They'll clear the way for my brother to get inside Newkirk. Together, we'll do whatever is necessary to kill this bastard."

"I suspected Walter was on our side."

She gives my hands a gentle squeeze before dropping them. "He may not be a born son of Rygard, but he's bled for this kingdom." There is a note of pride in her hushed voice. "He'll be loyal to you because you obviously love this kingdom to sacrifice everything for it."

"He will be rewarded for his loyalty," I assure her.

Excitement is a lightning strike in my veins when I realize how close we are to finally taking John's throne.

Eleanor flicks a nervous glance at the wall panel. "John is

sick, Rapunzel. He's dying. That's why he was desperate to find you."

"Yes, I suspected as much."

"He's gotten worse. Much worse." Her whole body shudders. "He came to me tonight to do his…business. While he was on top of me, he began coughing. Then spitting up blood. Then he collapsed. I had to call for his physician."

I notice the spatter of blood on her white sleeping gown. When I return my gaze to her somber face, I finally look hard enough through the dim light and note fresh bruises darkening her fair flesh. "Eleanor…"

She waves a hand through the air. "Even when at his weakest, John enjoys inflicting pain upon others almost as much as he relishes power."

"I'm sorry we didn't come sooner."

"No matter." She touches her fingertips to her cut bottom lip. "We're going to kill him, and that's enough for me. Thank God for the rule of hereditary succession, for I'll be glad when the crown is no longer mine." Absently, she touches her head, and I can almost feel the lifting of her burden and the weight of it transferring to me. "But we must act quickly because his health won't hold, and he's growing desperate."

God forgive me, but if ever a man deserves his death, it's King John of Rygard. "Can Sir Walter get to Quinn tonight?"

Eleanor thinks for a moment, then nods, "I believe so. The physician gave John a sleeping tonic. That will give us a few hours before he wakes."

"Perfect." When Eleanor rushes to leave, I clamp a hand around her arm to stop her. "I need yarrow, comfrey, woad, a pestle and mortar, and shears. And vials. Three of them. How fast can you get those for me? Can you get those to me?"

"Yes… We should have plenty in the apothecary… It won't be easy, but it can be done. Sir Walter will get them and pass them on to me. I'll deliver them to you." Then she gives me a peculiar look and whispers, "Whatever do you need them for?"

"Your brother taught me that all is fair in battle. I plan to give our men the upper hand."

No matter the cost.

No matter the pain.

No matter their refusal.

"Company's coming." Quinn's quiet announcement breaks the hush of the night.

"Some men seem to want to die," Dax drawls beside me. He pokes a stick into the small fire in the center of our tight camp. We're hidden deep in the forest outside Newkirk, yet well within the shadow of the fortress. "How many?"

Quinn sniffs the air. "Two." He inhales again. "No, one."

I lift a brow. "Scout?"

Sitting on the edge of a rock, his ass more off the large stone than on, Quinn closes his eyes. Tilts his head. Listens. Then he reopens those black eyes and scans the surrounding trees. "Walter."

"And he's alone?" Dax's surprise mirrors my own.

"He didn't strike me as a fool," I say. "Could be he's not here to fight."

A grunt rumbles out from deep within Quinn's chest. "Then he must be suicidal."

"But he gave us those two soldiers to kill. I don't know." Dax tosses his stick into the fire, causing the flames to snap and dance. "Something about the man… Doesn't seem right."

"He's wandering," Quinn tells us, one ear on us with the other on Sir Walter. "Probably walking in circles searching for us."

I nod at the fire. "Toss more wood on the flames and make it easier for him to find us."

Quinn lifts a brow. "Fuck that. Let him earn it."

Sir Walter obviously knows this forest well because he doesn't keep us waiting long. When he approaches our camp, the mad son of a bitch doesn't even have his sword palmed. It's nestled in its sheath, and his hands swing at his slides as if I don't have an arrow aimed at his heart, and Quinn isn't primed to tear out his throat.

"I admire his iron balls." I keep my eye trained on my target when I issue that praise.

"If you listen hard enough, you may hear them clank in his breeches." Dax twirls his sword in a wide arc, the showoff. "Shame we have to kill him."

"The sound you hear is the rocks banging around in your head." Then to our audacious visitor, "Got lost on your way to suck John's cock?"

Sir Walter ignores the barb and says, "If I was here for a fight, do you think I'd let you see me coming?"

Quinn grunts out a genuine laugh as he steps from the shadows. "Do you think I didn't track you a mile away?" He strolls right up to the brawny Captain of the Guard and presses his index and middle fingers to the front of the fur-lined brown cloak. "You have the stealth of a toddler."

Sir Walter rolls his eyes and smooths a hand down the front of his tunic as if brushing off Quinn's touch. "Unless you want to get us all killed and the princess tossed into the dungeon, I suggest you listen to what I have to say."

At the mention of Rapunzel, I lower my bow. "Speak."

In my peripheral vision, I see Dax sheath his sword. I replace the arrow in the quiver on my back as Dax says to him, "Looks like we aren't quite the barbarians. We're willing to be reasonable men."

"It's a miracle," Sir Walter snaps, and I want to applaud his sarcasm. To me, he says, "Rumor has it you're as good a shot as your father."

"Better," I admit, and to some, it might sound like boasting, but my father made sure I surpassed him in skill. He'd be proud that he'd succeeded in his task.

"Good to know," Sir Walter says with a meaningful nod. "May God bless us that we never need your aim, but I'm grateful to have it in our arsenal." Before I can remark, he adds, "Let's get to why I'm here. John is dying. Only his physician, Queen Eleanor, and by now, the princess knows this. John is desperate and will do whatever is necessary to stay alive and keep the crown on his head."

Quinn seizes Sir Walter by the throat and lifts him high enough that his toes scrape the ground. "Why should we believe you?"

"Because the queen sent me here herself," he grinds out.

"You're fucking lying," Quinn hisses.

"It's true." He fights to take his next breath, but Quinn is relentless. "I'm here to help you breach Newkirk."

"Give us a reason to trust you."

Dax taps Quinn on the shoulder. "Quinn? Put the man down and let him breathe."

Growling, Quinn releases Sir Walter with a shove. Sir Walter doubles over, hands on his thighs, gasping. Only once he's dragged in enough air does he straighten and glare at Quinn. "I'll allow that because you're the queen's brother. But *never* put your fucking hands on me again." He gulps in one more deep breath. "Your sister shared a story with me in the event you wouldn't believe me." His smirk is positively priceless. "When you were nine, you kissed a girl named Claire in the stable. Eleanor found you after, and—"

"Enough!" Quinn takes a menacing step forward. To his credit, Walter doesn't flinch. "You won't say more if you know what's good for you."

"So what if you kissed a girl behind a stable? I kissed a girl while hiding from her father in a pigsty," Dax confesses with a shrug.

Quinn gives the man his back as he turns to us. "I trust him. Let's go."

Shocked and more than mildly amused, I slip the arrow back in the quiver and sling the bow across my body. "No…" I hold up my hand and bring Quinn to a halt. Then I turn to the older man. "Finish the story."

Sir Walter's eyes flick to Quinn, then back to me. "Another time." Sir Walter digs into a pouch tied around his waist. He pulls out two vials and holds them out to Dax and me. "Princess Rapunzel instructed me to give these to you. I can't say that I'm surprised to learn she has the power to heal. Why else would John destroy his kingdom to find her? Always believed there was more to his madness than desperate, fatherly affection. Now, it all makes sense." He gestures to the vials still clutched in my hands. "She was generous enough to make one for me as well. But she knew you'd be angry. She asked me to remind you that you were the ones who repeatedly told her that victory must come at any cost."

Any cost to *us*. Not to *her*.

And angry?

No, try furious.

Rapunzel cut her hair—*her hair*. When this is over, first, I'm going to kiss her for all I'm worth…then I'm going to shake sense into the infernal woman for taking precious time off her life.

I snatch the vials from Sir Walter and stash it in the inner pocket of my wool jerkin. What I see are days. Weeks. Not the thick, yellow liquid. God only knows how much of Rapunzel's life is lost.

Dax takes his vial from me and tucks it in the pouch around his waist. "She shouldn't have done this." His voice is as brittle as the leaves beneath our feet.

"Listen, this breach must happen fast. After tonight, John will do whatever is necessary to force Princess Rapunzel to use her healing power on him. I don't know the extent of what she can do, but what we don't want is that man to regain his health."

"She can make him practically immortal," I mutter.

"Holy Mother of God…" Sir Walter whispers, horrified. "You tell me when you need a clear path to get inside Newkirk, and I'll have a small army waiting for you to help put Princess Rapunzel on the throne."

"Is tomorrow night too soon?"

"No time is too soon." Sir Walter glances over his shoulder at the massive castle looming like a distant, ominous smudge against the night sky. "There's a hidden tunnel set in the eastern wall. It's an escape route for the royal family to use during a siege. It's all but forgotten. Relatively unguarded. Enter there, and it will lead you to the royal wing of the castle. They're—"

"I know my way," I snap.

"As do I," Quinn adds.

While we never crossed paths at John's court, Quinn and I visited Newkirk enough to make our way around the castle blindfolded. Dax, not so much. He was a knight and therefore relegated to the garrison outside the keep. Although I don't trust anyone who isn't part of our immediate circle, we're stuck in a difficult position. Rapunzel and Eleanor are on the other side of those walls, leaving us no choice but to put their lives—and the success of our coup—in Sir Walter's hands.

"Tomorrow night then," Sir Walter spins and moves to hurry back to the castle, but Quinn leaps forward and clamps a hand around his arm. "Rapunzel." He grinds out her name. "And the queen. They are…well?"

Sir Walter's expression softens. "Aye. For now. But their safety is fleeting. We cannot wait."

I march to Sir Walter, Dax matching my stride with his hand resting on the hilt of his sword. His usual cheerful demeanor has been lost these past days we've camped in Newkirk's shadow. The weight of Rapunzel and Eleanor's lives—and the future of Rygard—are a heavy burden on our shoulders. "If anything happens to either of them between now and the morrow, I'm holding you personally responsible." I tear the dagger secured at my left hip from its small sheath and hover the tip near his cheek, just under his eye. "Am I at all unclear?"

"I have done everything within my power to protect those women." With admirable courage, Sir Walter slaps the blade away from his face. "I'm not the enemy."

"We're all on edge." Dax shoves me out of the way. Then he pries Quinn's fingers from Sir Walter's arm. "What Wren means to say is that we'll meet you at the rendezvous point tomorrow at the night guards' shift change. There. Better?"

"Be on time." Sir Walter walks backward. "We have a small window of opportunity. Miss it, and we're all dead—the queen included."

But not Rapunzel.

Her, John will keep alive.

To torment.

To use.

For the rest of his life—and because of her hair, he'll live a long twilight indeed.

And that's why when I look at Quinn, he's wearing a feral snarl, and there's a demonic gleam in his eyes as he lowers his chin and tilts his head to the left. "John dies tomorrow. As Rapunzel said, no matter the cost." Then to a retreating Sir

Walter he growls out, "Don't fuck us, old man. You won't like the consequences."

"Old man?" Sir Walter stops and, with a smirk, says. "At least I didn't trip over my feet and land in a pile of horseshit after my first kiss."

It takes every effort for Dax and me to keep our laughter quiet as we watch Sir Walter disappear into the forest. Goddamn, if the man didn't just endear himself to me because anyone who can fluster Quinn is worth his weight in salt.

Chapter Twenty

RAPUNZEL

The swallow of spiced wine skids down my throat like shards of glass. Keenly aware of my father beside me, I chew each bite of venison and every roasted vegetable until they're mush, nearly gagging on the texture. To help make the meal bearable, I listen with one ear to the din of conversations going around the twin tables below the dais while keeping up a discussion with Eleanor. John *graciously* allowed us to sit next to each other tonight in a public show of family unity. Privately, however, he has kept her under lock and key all day in the wake of his collapse. She, along with his physician and Sir Walter, has been the ones he's allowed to tend to him, keeping his illness secret.

I doubt he's aware I know he's sick.

Eleanor and I, along with Sir Walter, Cardinal Christopher Bram, and the king's physician, Aldo Fletcher, sit around the royal table. Each day at court is the same, with one running into the next. The hours are filled with hunting, games, music, and lavish meals. Most take place without him, with John's time spent secretly resting. He has never, however, missed an official audience. I've sat in during many of them, fascinated by the judicial process. Everyone from visiting nobility to farmers presented themselves to the king, with one dispute involving the questionable ownership of a cow. John considered this a minor skirmish. It wasn't insignificant to the men arguing over the proprietorship of the bovine when such an animal is crucial to the likelihood of one's family.

I always pretended to sew or draw when in reality, I listened and learned.

Learned how to be a worthy ruler.

The opposite of King John.

Unable to muster the fortitude to force down another morsel, I place my fork beside my plate and fiddle with the linen napkin on my lap. I'm startled when John's hand lands on my shoulder. He squeezes far harder than necessary to gain my attention. I hold in a wince and lift my lips in a sheepish grin. I swivel away from Eleanor and give this beast my full attention. "I'm sorry, Father, did you want something?"

"I would have a word with you." He keeps hold of me, his cunning glare slicing through me. "Privately."

It's challenging to maintain my false grin. "Of course."

"Now."

His tone brooks no argument. Placing my napkin on my plate, I push away from the table. Sir Walter shoots to his feet, but John instructs him to stay with the queen. Eleanor asks if she may join us, but a single stern look from her husband has her bowing her head and lowering her eyes. Her guard sets his large hands on her shoulders to keep her in the chair. He has the audacity to smirk. The bruises on her face are a spectacle of pain under the glow of the torchlight.

Not a person lingers their gaze too long on her, as if by ignoring the obvious, they can ignore the abuse. But *I* see. When Eleanor strode into the hall for tonight's meal, each member of John's court could not deny it, to themselves at least—that their queen suffers at the tortuous hands of their liege.

Respectfully, John's courtiers rise along with us. Laughing at their eagerness to please, the king bids them to retake their seats. "Eat and be merry, friends. The night has exhausted Princess Rapunzel. I would walk my daughter to her room."

John takes my hand, cradling it. For all intents and purposes, it looks like a loving gesture. In fact, he's all but crushing the bones of my fingers with surprising strength as he guides me from the table. My feet drag, and my stomach feels full of stones as I follow his lead into the quiet hall. One guard standing sentry closes the door after us, then falls in step as we walk in tense silence down the corridor. He wisely keeps a fair distance.

Shadows dance like demons in the muted glow of the flames flickering from the wall sconces as we head toward the steep steps that lead to the second level of the keep. My father, I realize, is not much taller than me—barely average height and painfully thin. I wonder why I haven't noticed this sooner or why I didn't see until now how gaunt his face is and how pale his lips are. Perhaps because, in my mind, he's a monster. The truth is, John of Rygard has deteriorated into a frail husk of a man whose shoulders have stopped from the burden of his sickness.

From the burden of his sins.

John has yet to release my hand, and I have to bite back a wince at the pain radiating across each finger. I want to spit in his face. Spew all the vile names at him that sit bitterly on my tongue. But I don't because Eleanor assured me that Quinn, Wren, and Dax are, even now, preparing to breach Newkirk. Sir Walter visited them himself. Personally handed them the vials filled with the elixir I mixed for them. I didn't take much hair—just a few sporadic strands for each man. Protection should they fall injured.

We reach the stairs, and he finally releases me with a shove. Compels me to walk in front of him, his presence behind me oppressive. He may be ill, but his unpredictability is no less terrifying.

Then he clamps his hand around my arm and pulls me to my room, with my heart a painful beat inside my chest. Does he know? Did Sir Walter betray us? I'll kill him myself. Both of them. It's the only way—

"Wait for me out here. I'll be but a moment," John instructs the guard. Finally, he frees me, and I rub my arm where he gripped me. He slams the door, the bang as loud as a clap of thunder. I brace for the lightning strike of his fury. "I've been more than patient with you. But I've reached the limit of my tolerance."

Feigning ignorance, I cross my arms over my chest in a protective stance. "I'm sure I don't know what you mean."

He coughs. Blood speckles his hand when he removes it from his mouth. Muttering a curse, he whips his palm across his thigh, smearing the drops of red into the blue satin of his breeches. "Don't play ignorant with me, Rapunzel. You know exactly what I mean." He lunges at me with shocking speed. "This." He grabs my hair and yanks on the golden plait. "You're going to give me the magic infused in your fucking hair."

"Stop it." I try to pry my hair from his hand, but his grip is tight. "You're scaring me."

"Good." He tugs the braid again before releasing it.

As I back away, I stumble over my feet but quickly right my footing. "I can't."

"You mean you *won't*," he roars. "But you *will*." When he sways and releases a cacophony of grating coughs, he hunches over and grips the mattress to steady himself. Only once the racking hacks end does he straighten and square his shoulders, struggling to regain his lost dignity. "I would rather have you freely share the magic with me, but I will take it from you by force if I must."

And there it is.

The threat I knew was forthcoming.

Thank God Sybil took me from this monster when I was

born. The things he would have done to me... The torture I would have suffered at his hands is unimaginable.

I give him what I hope is a sympathetic expression even as hatred burns a hot path through my veins. "I understand you're ill, and I want to help you. But each time I use the magic, it comes at a grave cost."

Morbid curiosity demands I hear his response, however callous it will be.

Also, I need to buy time for my men to breach the castle. Every moment wasted grants them the precious moments they need. Sir Walter's men wait for his order to take control of the garrison elsewhere within these walls. Anticipation crackles within me, a slow building deep within my belly that radiates up to my chest until each breath comes in short, excited bursts.

To John, I must appear frightened.

The fool.

He straightens his spine, coughs, then takes my measure. Where there was a fire in his eyes when I first arrived, there is now a...dullness. "What care do I have for the cost to you?"

You, indeed, are a cruel son of a bitch

Of course, I keep this thought to myself as I cross to the hearth. I appreciate that there's always a fire burning to keep the damp and the cold at bay. Sadly, the mesmerizing flame can't fend off the chill caused by John's callousness.

"There are items I need to make an elixir. Mugwort. Anise. Lavender. St. John's Wort." I rattle off herbs that, although medicinal, are useless when mixed with my hair. "Also, I ask for time to prepare myself for the pain."

"Prepare yourself while I rot with disease? You are a selfish bitch," John roars. I don't realize how close he is until he spins me around, the shock of his slap sending me to the ground. But the kick to the stomach knocks the air from my lungs. Gasping, I throw one arm around my midsection. Fling my other over my face. I'm too startled to remember my newfound instinct to fight back. He towers over me, jabbing his index finger at me. "I'll grant you one night, Rapunzel. You have one fucking night to *prepare yourself* while my physician gathers the herbs you require." For a moment, I fear he'll kick me again, but he doesn't. "My patience only goes so far, even for you. Either willingly give me what I need or so help me God, I'll have my men hold you down while I personally cut every strand of hair off your stubborn fucking head."

I push down the pain, anger, and hurt and shuffle to my feet. Scraping up all my dignity, I notch up my chin to meet his livid gaze. "That is the first and last time you will *ever* strike me. Next time you try, I will cleave your hand from your wrist."

He narrows those angry eyes on me. "You dare to—"

"Yes, I dare." I could kill him… And risk everything before all the pieces are in place because I couldn't keep my temper in check. No, I'm smarter than that. Training at Dyhurst wasn't solely about how to defend myself. It was also how to control a situation. John believes *he's* in command here. In truth, he is a puppet. I hold the strings. "I am Rygard's princess. No one lays their hands on me." This man speaks a language of violence. I must do the same. Anything less will be taken as a weakness. He must view me as a worthy opponent, or I may as well surrender to him and walk myself into his dungeon. "For the sake of this kingdom, swear you will not threaten to take from me what I will freely give you, and we will have peace between us."

His eyes are full of suspicion. "No trickery, Rapunzel."

"No trickery. You are my father. Of course I will do this for you." With effort, I keep the disgust from my voice. "But not at the tip of a sword."

John mulls this over a moment, his coveting, curious gaze locked on my hair. "Explain this…" He waves a hand through the air. "Agony."

I pull the heavy braid over my shoulder and run my hand

along the grooves of the plait. "The pain equals severing a limb when the strands are cut. It's fleeting but excruciating."

John rubs his forehead. Stifles a cough. Then he tugs the front of his blue tunic in place. Smooths a hand over the buttery brocade to ensure it lays perfectly over his torso to maintain an air of nobility. "Sybil's magic always came at a cost. It killed your mother to give you life, and that's why I took her tongue. Now, she can't infect the world with her foul art."

The ease with which he says this sends a shot of loathing up my spine. "You did Rygard a great service by locking her safely inside your dungeon."

I want to spit the taste of that lie out of my mouth.

John keeps his cynical stare on me, seeking, I'm sure, a fracture in my performance. What this bastard doesn't realize is that a lifetime spent in near-isolation taught me how to master my emotions.

"Did I?" One side of his mouth lifts in a sardonic grin. "Then after we take care of…this…" He gestures to his failing body. "Together, we'll see to Sybil."

"She kept me chained to the tower for twenty-four years." I match his sinister grin. "That witch owes me my life."

A hint of tension eases from him. "You give me what I need, and I'll consider relaxing your restrictions."

Indeed—I thought he said I wasn't his prisoner.

"Go back to the hall, Father. Attend to your friends." Although it disgusts me, I embrace him and feel how frail he is in my arms. "Come the morrow, everything will be as it should be. I promise you."

I've fed this man many lies since the day Sir Walter brought me to Newkirk, but this vow is the first truth I've spoken to King John. It's an oath I make, not to him, but to Rygard.

Because in a few hours, John will be dead, and this kingdom will finally be free.

QUINN

True to his word, Sir Walter cleared the way for our entry into Newkirk. The narrow walls of the tunnel band around me as we travel toward the keep. Our footfalls are drumbeats. Wren and Dax's breathing behind me are gale winds. Their racing hearts are the deafening claps of frantic thunder. Damp, stale air permeates my black leather breeches and matching, heavy jerkin to seep straight to the void where my soul should live.

Above all, Rapunzel and Eleanor are beacons guiding me down this endless, murky corridor. Their energy tugs me forward, cutting through the darkness.

In enemy territory, I keep my sword palmed. I can't wipe the smirk off my face when I remember the night beside the lake with Rapunzel.

There's an arched wooden doorway at the end of the tunnel. I give a pull. Locked from the other side. Fuck. If Sir Walter betrayed us, I'll kill him last. Kill him slowest. Make his death the messiest, and make it hurt the most.

But I smell him on the other side.

Wren's hand lands on my shoulder. "Problem?"

I shake my head. "No." Then I give the door the faintest rap of my knuckles.

He answers back with a tap. Then there's a whisper so low, I need to strain to hear it, "A moment."

"He's there," I rasp. "Waiting."

Time crawls over us in an excruciatingly slow march. I listen to the activity in the hallway. Feet shuffling over the stone floor. The echo of unfamiliar voices. Beads of sweat accumulate on my upper lip as each passing moment slides into the next as frustration builds into a frenzy.

"Quinn!"

Wren's voice calms me. "What? I'm fine," I hiss.

Skeptical, he narrows his worried brown eyes on me. "You fucking better be."

Dax squeezes around Wren. He settles a heavy—and reassuring—hand on my back. "The man said he's fine, Wren. Leave it be."

But I glance at the dead space down the corridor, and for a moment, I swear I see the shadow of the demon who owns my soul watching us.

Is it here as an omen to predict our failure…or because, win or lose, I'm dead either way?

Whatever it may be, I have no time to contemplate it because the door opens. Muted torchlight light floods the corridor. Sir Walter waves us inside the main hallway. We push past him with memories from my family's years here flashing unbidden through my mind. Pleasant memories of my mother and siblings pave the way for the reminder of Stephan and my father plotting against my sister.

"The courtiers linger in the hall," Sir Walter explains as he leads us to a steep, darkened stairway. "But John has already retired with his mistress. My men are securing the garrison as we speak."

Perfect.

We climb the stairs, and the hallway is empty when we reach the top. Sir Walter points down one length of the corridor. "The queen is there. Princess Rapunzel's chamber is that way." He gestures in the other direction, where the passageway splits. "We didn't have time to clear their guards."

Dax swings his sword in a wide arc. Anticipation lights his eyes. "Not a problem. I've got Rapunzel."

"I'll see to the queen." Sir Walter motions down the last direction. "John is this way. Hurry."

As if we don't remember *exactly* where the King of Rygard's chambers are in this massive fortress. Quinn and Wren break away from the others, with Dax racing off one way and Sir Walter in the other. Wren and I take off toward John. I follow the wheezing, indrawn breaths, and shuttering exhales of a sick man mingling with the feminine whimpers and muffled sobs coming from the last room at the end of the hallway.

I shake off the abhorrent sensation of the demon's breath blowing hot across my neck as I slice through the soldier guarding the door. Then I kick open the last barrier that stands between John and us. The metal sliding lock snaps, and the door slams open. Undaunted, John is already off the woman. Hastily, he tugs on his breeches. His white shirt hangs loosely around his body. He dissolves into a coughing fit.

Gone is the robust sportsman who never missed a hunt. This man stinks of decay. His rotting body is half the size it was when last I was at court. His clothing drapes on his frail frame like a child wearing his father's garb. And when he finally regains his breath, he still can't muster the dignity he once had.

Wren, ever the gentleman, acts fast to cover the terrified girl cowering on the bed. Barely old enough to be called a woman. "Go," he tells her.

Her chin quivering and tears raining down her cheeks, she shoots a glare at John, then spits at his feet. She turns her wide, wild eyes on Wren. "I hope you kill him."

With one hand clutching the blanket around her body and the other slapped over her mouth, she dashes from the room in a mess of tangled brown hair. Wren kicks the door closed. It can't lock now, thanks to me breaking it, but at least we have some semblance of privacy with this son of a bitch.

"If you wanted an audience with me, you didn't have to sneak in like rats through a sewer," John sneers.

"Audience? No." Wren walks a circle around John. "We're here for a reckoning."

John *tsks*. "I don't think so, but I appreciate that you've exposed disloyalty within my ranks. It will be a pleasure to use this as an example of what happens when you fuck with the crown."

My ink-black fingers tighten around my sword's hilt. With my free hand, I grab the collar of my shirt and jerkin and yank them down to expose my collarbone. To show him the demon's marks that creep down my neck to disappear beneath my clothing. "Look at me, you piece of shit." I release my clothing. The need to rip out his heart hums through me. "I'm going to enjoy sending you to Hell."

John smirks as if he has the right to be arrogant. "I wonder if Eleanor agrees."

Choosing not to fall victim to his taunt, I close the distance between us. Wren and I are in control here, and when I grab John by the chin and force him to look deep into my eyes, I make damn sure he understands this. "For the pain you caused this kingdom, I want you on your knees begging for your life."

I allow John to slap my hand away. "The way your sister begs for hers?"

Fuck it. I tried to be pragmatic.

The backhand sends John to his knees. Didn't I say I wanted him there? He should have complied nicely, now look. I'm upset. His mouth bleeding, and he's coughing again. What's Wren saying? Something about how John deserves more than a slap to the face for the murder of his mother. I must agree. Mothers are sacred, and this bastard killed Mary Kincaid when he ordered his men to destroy Leeds Village.

John pushes to his feet, his legs unsteady. He jabs a finger at Wren. "Your parents betrayed me! Mary and Percy knew Sybil took my daughter. Your father was my friend, yet he conspired to steal my daughter from me!"

Wren appears as confused as I am at John's outburst. With eyes narrowed, he levels his sword at John. "What nonsense do you spew, old man?"

"You think you know everything, but you know nothing! Percy claimed friendship and loyalty to me all those years, but it was a cruel ruse. Your father and Sybil conspired to steal that cursed child from me if my beloved wife perished in childbirth. They took Rapunzel and hid her in Blythe. It was no coincidence he retired to Leeds. He wanted to watch over Rapunzel." He dabs blood from his mouth. "I gave your traitorous father a merciful death. What I should have done was stick his head."

"You son of a bitch," Wren shouts as he charges John.

Because that's what the bastard wants.

Grabbing Wren's arm, I stop him. "Control yourself," I warn him, to which Wren takes a deep, calming breath. The resistance eases out of him. "This is him asking for an easy death. Don't give it to him."

Wren nods, and right when I'm about to demand Rapunzel and Eleanor be brought to us, I *feel* it… The faintest trickle of unease slithers up my spine. The sound of footfalls follows an… unnerving…sensation emanating from the hallway. Two pairs. Marching toward the chamber. Two heartbeats. One races with the anticipation of battle. One thunders with fear. There's feminine energy buried beneath an aggressive masculine force.

I whip my gaze to John. His arrogance says so much—too much—without uttering a single fucking word.

"Stop!" I don't know who I yell this at or what I'm

demanding to cease. Maybe for those fucking footsteps to halt. For John to wipe that goddamn sneer off his miserable fucking face. For my dread to loosen its chokehold on me. I don't know. Just…stop.

John's wheezing laughter shakes his disease-ridden body. "Fools!" He shrieks. "I am *King*. I have eyes and ears every-where within these walls. No one breathes inside this castle without me knowing. Did you not think one of my soldiers would tell me you were planning this silly little coup with Walter? Now stand aside, or my man will start cutting Rapunzel's hair." Then he looks right at me. "Or would you chance your speed against how much hair she will lose before you open that door and wrench the shears from his hands? It's your choice, of course, but if I were you, I would choose wisely. After all, we don't know how much life each strand costs her."

Fuck.

The sadistic bastard's smug expression makes me want to take that chance.

But I can't. Not when I know the pain will cause her. Victory at any cost, yes, but we're not at that point.

Not fucking yet.

Hopefully, it won't get that far.

"Open the goddamn door," I growl at Wren.

He mutters a string of the foulest curses but hauls open the heavy wooden door. Rapunzel is shoved inside the chamber, and it's the first time we've seen her in weeks. Her exquisite face upends my world. It takes everything I am not to run to her and yank her from the soldier's arms. All I can this is: *God, I've missed this woman.*

Her hair falls around her like a shroud, making her appear small. Her bare feet make her seem vulnerable. When I spot a spray of blood on the cream-colored sleeping gown, I study her from head to foot, seeking a source of her injuries. Finding none, I glare at the son of a bitch behind her, searching him first from the metal shears near her hair, then to his bloody nose. Seems our woman put up a good fight.

Rapunzel holds her head high, rage reflected in her eyes as she sweeps the room. But she doesn't dare move her head. Not one inch, lest those twin blades snap even a single strand. Only her eyes move, softening when they land on Wren and me. "I'm sorry," she whispers.

"You are a duplicitous and treasonous bitch." To the soldier, he shouts, "Cut it." But the order dissolves into a cough.

Wren shouts, "No!"

"Motherfucker," I roar as I lunge forward.

Too late.

Rapunzel's agonized scream cracks across the chamber. I may be fast, and I may be strong, but I can't stop those shears. The weight of my failure takes me to the ground. I drop to my knees, frozen, staring at the horrific puddle of golden hair pooled at her tiny bare feet.

She collapses in a mangled mess. Oh, my fucking God. What did they do to her? The crown of her head is choppy brown, the underside long and golden. Panting and sweating, she ignores the tears that rain down her face as she reaches up with trembling hands to finger what's left on her head. Then she heaves, spitting up bile and saliva. With wild eyes, she gathers the bits of hair and examines the loose locks as if what just happened hasn't yet clicked in her mind. Then she lets it filter through her fingers like sand before rocking back and forth, crying as her pain fills the room like a heavy cloud.

In my peripheral vision, I see Wren charge John. He has the fucker captive at the tip of his sword. "You're fucking dead."

"She comes with me," John threatens, laughing like a madman.

No, I don't fucking think so.

I pop to my feet. Focus my attention on the soldier brandishing those shears. He lowers them toward Rapunzel's head. I didn't sacrifice my soul to stand here and do nothing while my woman dies.

With a swipe of my sword and a flick of my wrist, I open the soldier's throat. I watch with savage satisfaction as his blood seeps out in a deep, crimson rivulet down the front of his tunic. He drops the shears with a gasp and backs away from Rapunzel. Chokes on a mouthful of blood that splatters out to spray my face. He stumbles over his feet to slide in his blood, grasping at his severed neck. Finally, he falls, landing in a heap, dead.

Livid, John points at me and opens his mouth to say something, but he isn't dictating the situation. We are. "I want you to beg for your miserable life."

"Go fuck yourself, Quinn Redgrave," John sneers.

"How brave of you," I say with a nasty laugh. "Brave, but incredibly stupid."

I'm about to sheath my sword—I intend to rip this bastard's heart out—but more footfalls thunder down the corridor. They stop at the threshold, and before my warning to Wren even leaves me, he's already yanking a weak and whimpering Rapunzel to her feet. He shoves her behind him, putting his body between her and the doorway.

Between her and whatever threat may burst through that door.

But it's not a threat. At least that's not what I see first— because I can't look past the familiar green eyes staring back at me.

Eleanor.

She's grown, but she's still a tiny thing. Still dark-haired and full of fire. Last I saw her, she was two years younger. Lifetimes more innocent. The naive girl Edgar Redgrave and Stephan of Glasburg gave to John as a bride is gone. There is only a battered woman saturated in soul-crushing pain and misery, and when she reaches for me, she's tugged back by a soldier threatening her with a dagger at her throat.

I'm going to kill him too.

"I repeat, I am king," John taunts. He smooths his clothes. Runs his fingers through his hair. All to regain his lost dignity in front of the handful of soldiers that file into the room.

The soldier nicks Eleanor's neck when I charge John. It's a warning that stops me cold.

"Not even you're quick enough to kill us before one of my men takes your sister or Rapunzel with us." John's laughter rings out as he clasps his hands behind his back. "Seems that puts us at an impasse." He looks down with disgust, pulls back his leg, and kicks the dead soldier at his feet. "Useless," he mutters. But to me, "At least you are a worthy opponent, as one would expect from a Redgrave."

"No!" Eleanor's strained scream damn near shatters me. "Please, John, don't do this. Please, I beg you."

He gives her a sardonic grin. "I'll certainly have you begging, my dear wife. I promise you that. Oh, yes, I'll enjoy keeping you obedient while your brother watches."

Pushed too far, I strike, swinging my sword with swift and lethal precision that slices my way through four soldiers. Through the bang of blades and the screams of the men I fell, I hear John's single command.

Issued calmly.

Eerily concise.

"Kill her."

I whip around in time to see the soldier holding the blade to my sister's neck nod. The dagger glints in the firelight. I lunge toward him, and I watch as he gasps, the dagger slipping from his hand. His eyes are wide as his chin falls to rest on his chest. Glazed eyes settle on his chest as if searching for something that isn't there. I stab a shallow strike through his heart and grin over the dying man's shoulder at Sir Walter. His blade dug into the soldier's back.

"No one touches our queen," Sir Walter hisses.

This man just earned my eternal loyalty.

Indeed.

Sir Walter yanks his weapon free, and we slaughter three more soldiers together. Fissions of energy slither across my nerves when I feel a familiar presence join us. *Dax.* I glance to my right and see he's just killed someone who tried to attack Sir Walter from behind.

The clash of swords is so loud I'm positive everyone in the castle hears the commotion. We only have moments to kill John and take control of the castle and its garrison.

With time pressing down on us, I spin, searching for my sister. I don't see her right away, but when I do, she's not watching the fight. Her hands cover her mouth, and her expression is contorted in horror. I follow her gaze to John and see a soldier's dagger in his hand. Triumph is written all over his face.

I drop my eyes and…

Oh, my fucking God.

Rapunzel cradles a mortally wounded Wren in her lap. Over her is a soldier. He holds shears to what's left of her mangle hair. Wren's hands are around his own bleeding throat. Too much blood oozes from between his fingers.

John grabs Eleanor and hauls her across the room, nearly tripping over dead bodies. He jabs the dagger under her chin. "Stand down, or they both die." A quick bout of unrestrained coughing follows his bellow.

"I don't think you'll kill them," I grind between clenched teeth.

Please be fucking bluffing.

"Fine," he snaps. "Eleanor it is."

Even as I unstick my feet from the floor and dive for John, Eleanor's voice—her lovely voice—knocks the wind out of me. "I love you, Quinn."

She just said goodbye.

No, no, fucking no! My sister doesn't die tonight.

"Stop!" It's Rapunzel's ragged, guttural cry that halts John's hand. "Please, no more."

"What's that, Daughter? You have something to say?" John mocks her with his cool tone. The dagger in his hand trembles from the strain of his weakened muscles.

"Enough." Rapunzel reaches into Wren's jerkin. Fishes the vial of elixir from his pocket. She opens the glass vial and presses it to Wren's mouth. Almost instantly, his throat begins the arduous healing process. I know because mine did the same after she used her magic to repair my injury. "This is what you want, John. All this fighting… All this death. I'll give this magic to you, but you must call off your soldiers. Free Eleanor and Sybil. Allow Quinn, Wren, and Dax to leave Rygard, and I'll give you what's left of my hair."

"Fuck that, no. Rapunzel, no." I don't know what's real or what's pretense.

"Little Captive." Rapunzel swings her watery gaze at Dax. "Don't do this."

She squeezes her eyes closed for only a moment. Then she opens them, her smile small and sad. She strokes Wren's bloody hair from his face. "It always had to happen like this."

"Fucking don't, Rapunzel," I growl.

"Quinn, please." She blinks away the tears that glisten in her beautiful eyes. Then she sets her chin at a determination lift and meets her father's ruthless glare. "I yield, John."

'I don't yield. Ever.'

Rapunzel never gave up. Even the tower couldn't defeat her.

If that didn't break her…

I raise my hands in surrender. "As you wish, Rapunzel," I sneer with as much venom as I can muster. "But I hope you know this lying fucking bastard won't honor his word, and when he betrays us, it'll be on your miserable fucking soul."

For good measure, I spit on the floor.

"Silence him!" John shouts, and the remaining soldiers come toward me.

"I dare you," I growl.

They wisely back away.

But Dax, being a rowdy prick, has to get one last swipe in and *accidentally* stabs the soldier closest to him. He shrugs. "Sorry. I was already swinging."

He was not.

The soldier falls to the ground, dead.

"See? I cannot trust you!" John yells.

Without moving her head, Rapunzel darts her gaze to me, then back to John. Something in her eyes warns me this won't go well—for me. "Allow me to prove my loyalty."

With that dagger jerky against my sister's throat, John glowers at Rapunzel. "What can you possibly do to prove such a thing to me?

"Eliminate a threat in your kingdom to seal our truce."

John is hesitant. The tension is brutal until finally, he says, "Fine, Rapunzel, you have my word."

Which is worth absolutely nothing.

"Order your man to free her hair."

Again, John hesitates, but also again, he eventually agrees. I'm sure for no other reason than curiosity. Rapunzel pushes herself to her feet. She's soaked with Wren's blood as she slips a dagger from its sheath at his hip. Every muscle in my body goes taut as she walks toward me. My gut coils because I can practically read her thoughts.

I'm the threat who must play dead.

She gives me no warning before plunging the blade into my left eye.

"Next time, take the eye."

She remembered.

Eleanor's scream echoes around me as agony rips through my face. The nauseating squish of the blade slicing my eyeball drowns out all other sounds. The grotesque tug as Rapunzel pulls out the blade turns my stomach, and I nearly disgrace myself by vomiting all over my feet. The dagger hits the ground as I choke on a strangled gasp and stagger back. My hands fly to my face, blood blinding the eye she left perfectly intact.

"Poisoned," Rapunzel says. Of course this is a lie. "In case we ever had to put him down."

Like a mongrel.

With pain resonating throughout my entire skull, I make a good show of things by grabbing the nearing object. Purposely wobble. Let out a theatric groan. Someone laughs. Turning, I let go of whatever I'm holding. Dramatically stumble over a dead soldier. Slam my back against the wall and slide down to the floor in a haze of very real pain bleeding all over the stone floor.

This is the first and last time I will lie at John's feet.

Chapter Twenty-Two

RAPUNZEL

All the days of my life led me to this moment.

Pain and sorrow and loneliness made me strong.

The years in the tower gave me grim determination.

Wren, Quinn, and Dax's love is the support I need as I inch toward my father. "I've learned one vital lesson since Wren took me from the tower. Would you like to know what it is?" I step over Quinn to position myself closer to John and Eleanor. A wave of nausea rolls through me as I avoid the carnage that litters the chamber floor.

Behind me, Dax and Sir Walter move with me, acting as a wall that conceals Wren from John's manic view.

"How to kill that blasphemous creature?" He gestures with a nod at Quinn." He rolls his eyes at the firm set of my jaw and disgusted flare of my nostrils—not to mention Eleanor's tortured sob. "Fine. Tell me quick, Rapunzel." John jostles his wife when he shifts her in his arms, the dagger scraping against her throat. "I would put an end to this wretched night."

"Actually, John, I learned a little blood makes for a big

distraction." I take advantage of John's confusion and surge forward to tug Eleanor away from him.

John reaches for Eleanor but grasps at the empty air as we jump out of the way. Dax and Sir Walter part, and there's Wren, lying on his back with head lifted, bow primed. Gaze locked on Rygard's stunned king.

Only his fingers move, dispatching the arrow. It pierces John's left eye, mirroring how Percy Kincaid killed Henry.

Wren, after all, was trained by the best.

Thrown back by the impact, John drops the dagger. Before his body hits the ground, Quinn pops to his feet, bloody eye and all. He grabs John by the throat. Dangles the gasping, dying man like a broken doll above the ground. Yanks him close, nose to nose. "Not yet, you son of a bitch."

Then Quinn plunges his right hand deep into John's chest.

The crack of bone and sloppy wetness mingles with John's guttural grunts and gurgles. Then the king's body jerks. Once. Twice. Slumps in Quinn's hold as his bloody hand emerges heart gripped in his first. "I'll see you in fucking Hell."

Drained of his strength, Quinn tosses John aside like trash. The heart slips out of his hand, and when he sways, Eleanor is there, wrapping her arms around her brother. She's crying, her neck bleeding from where John pressed the sword's tip to the delicate flesh. Then she glares at me as if *I'm* the enemy. "How could you?"

Frantically, I shake my head. "I had to." Again, my stomach heaves at the lingering feel of the blade sinking into Quinn's eyeball.

"I'm fine, Little Badger." He blinks a few times as if clearing his vision, his mutilated eye growing back. "It was a sound plan." He kisses the top of her head. "I've missed you."

She's gazing up at him in adoration, her arms still locked around his waist as if she's afraid to let him go. "I've missed you as well."

"Come here, Princess."

I'm breathless when I reach him, and Quinn hooks a finger under my chin and forces me to look up at him. "You took the eye."

"I took the eye," I repeat.

His expression darkens when he passes his gaze over my head. I can only imagine what a mess I am. "I need to sit down before I fall down," he groans without taking his eyes off my mangled hair.

He drops to the edge of the bed with Eleanor practically fused to his side. His eye is already healing, but he's covered in blood. His. John's. The men he's killed.

With one last soldier left standing, the coward surrenders. Dax, however, doesn't show the man who held my hair in those shears any mercy. Then, with a fist to his heart and deep bow, Sir Walter takes his leave to free Sybil and gather what remains of the garrison.

Rygard is mine.

We won.

But I find no joy in this victory—especially when Dax musses what's left of my hair. "You're a mess, Little Captive." He pulls me into his arms and hugs me so tightly he squeezes the air out of me. "I love you too much." He rains kisses all over my face. "I was terrified we were going to lose you." His next kiss is so tender I can't stop the tears that spill down my cheeks. I cling to him, breathing him in, savoring him.

And then he's gone, and Wren is there. My Wren. The boy who found me in the tower. Who I've loved since I was twelve. The man who once hated me but ultimately saved me. Who freed me. And who is kissing me as if I am his next breath.

This man who nearly died in my arms.

Oh, God…

I love these men with all of myself. With every part of me.

Then Wren touches my hair with a reverence that tears my heart to pieces. They'll see the loss of half my life staring back at them whenever they look at me. They'll spend the rest of our lives preserving what's left of my golden hair.

That is no life at all.

I pull away from Wren and turn to Dax. "The vial I gave you… Did you use it?"

"Fuck no," Dax says with a smirk. "Unlike these two," he motions to Wren and Quinn, who are literally bloody messes. "I kept myself alive during this fight."

Thank God. "May I see it, please?"

Dax fishes inside the pocket of his jerkin for the vial. "See? Told you. It's full."

Perfect.

I pick up the dropped shears and act quickly before anyone realizes what I'm about to do. I fist what's left of my long hair. Someone shouts my name. Someone else yells. Then Quinn dives for me. But he's a breath too late. I squeeze the shears. The blades cut. Oh, sweet God in Heaven, they cut. Agony pulls a scream from me as every nerve in my body ignites with pain. I think the shears slip from my fingers, but agony clouds my mind. I drop to the floor…

But I don't collide with the stone.

Quinn catches me. "Oh, God. Fuck. What did you do, Rapunzel?"

His wail resonates throughout the room, with chaos making everything a blur. I have to close my eyes, and in the darkness, the pain ebbs. It's calm here. Warm. But lonely. So very lonely. Like being dropped in the middle of a vast, cold nothingness.

"The elixir," Dax bellows. "Here. Give her the fucking elixir."

I open my eyes, and pain slams back into my body. I roar out a cry. Grasp for…something. I don't know. Quinn's face hovers above me. Then there's Wren, and he pries open my jaw. Dax pours the elixir between my lips. It slides down my throat like a hundred white-hot flames searing me from the inside out.

"You better live long enough for me to fucking kill you for this, Princess."

I want to laugh at Quinn's asinine comment, but I can't. I'm too busy choking on the elixir. Or am I burning alive? Is this dying? Yes. This is dying, I'm sure of it, and it's awful. I have to close my eyes again and slip back into the void. Only now, I'm not alone. Quinn's demon is here, and he's angry.

At me.

'You stole him.'

I damn sure did.

'One more truth, and he's your monster to keep.'

He damn sure is.

Now, go away and leave us alone because I'm not ready to die, and you can't have Quinn's soul. It's his to keep—but his heart belongs to me.

The demon's laughter—its wicked, heinous laughter—follows me back to consciousness.

"There you are, Rapunzel. Don't you dare leave us." Dax's voice penetrates the blackness. It coaxes me awake, and the pain is gone when I blink my eyes open. I'm *very* much alive—and surrounded by three *fur*ious renegades. "There's our girl." Dax smooths a hand through my hair. "Have I told you I've always preferred brunettes?"

I cough out a laugh at the same time Quinn punches Dax in the face. While Dax rubs his cheek, Wren helps me sit up. All around me, my golden hair is withering. Dying on the floor.

As it should.

My days of hiding are over. I want to live a normal, mortal life. With my men. My renegades. We fought for this. We damn —*I*—damn well deserve it. We may be battered and bloody and have a kingdom to rebuild, but we won the battle and defeated a king.

But our newly acquired responsibilities can wait until tomorrow because tonight…

Tonight is for us.

Chapter Twenty-Three

DAX

Behold, our queen.

Look at her.

A work of art.

It was Wren's idea to have her wear the crown.

My idea to strip her naked first.

Outside this chamber, Newkirk teams with activity as the staff, led by Sir Walter, scrambles to clean up the mess of our coup. Including the disposal of John's body. We expected resistance from the remainder of the three-hundred-strong garrison. More than half fought alongside our allies to help secure the garrison. Those who opposed… Their deaths convinced any lingering reluctant soldiers to lay down their weapons and swear allegiance to Rygard's rightful queen.

But it was when Cardinal Bram dropped to one knee and proclaimed that Rapunzel was a blessing upon this land that the courtiers fell in step and offered her their loyalty as well.

It certainly helped our cause that the cardinal also had been dear friends with Percy Kincaid. He never forgave John for Percy's murder.

Our first order of business was to bring Sybil up from the

dungeon. The poor old woman couldn't even walk. John, the prick, beat the witch damn near to death. After a brief reunion, Sybil was taken to the infirmary, where she will be cared for by the royal physician.

Aldo hated the king as well.

There was plenty of that sentiment to go around this kingdom.

With Sybil under the physician's care and Sir Walter managing the army, all else can wait until the morrow because the new queen of Rygard is ours for the rest of this night.

And that fucking crown—handed to Rapunzel by Cardinal Bram—looks damn good atop those bouncy brown curls.

I wasn't lying when I told Rapunzel I preferred brunettes. God's teeth, but I thought she was beautiful as a blonde. The woman is enchanting with dark hair. I even like it short. It reveals more of her lovely face.

Fuck, how I missed this face.

"Come here to me, Little Captive."

A vision in the fire blazing in the hearth across the room, Rapunzel, fresh from a bath, holds her head steady as she saunters toward me. The gentle swing of her hips doesn't mesmerize only me but also holds the attention of Wren and Quinn. This tiny woman hopelessly charmed us. This stubborn woman—who scared me to death when she gave up the last of her magic. My heart stopped when those shears severed what remained of those golden strands. We lost her, for a time, our Rapunzel. And even though I held the vial that contained her elixir, I never experienced pure terror as I did tonight when I watched that golden hair flutter to the floor.

My body still hums with that horror right down to my fingertips. I have to kiss her again to get the flavor of fear out of my mouth and replace it with her.

Somehow, her mortality makes her all the more fascinating.

"I love you," she whispers against my mouth.

I wrap my arms around her waist. Hold her so close, her heartbeat drums against my chest. "You have no fucking idea how much I love you." Then I kiss her again because once wasn't enough.

I'm a greedy man.

The worry and tension, and fury that built up over the weeks we were separated drain from me. Dissipate on the air. Let it dissolve into the ether until it's no longer a living entity between us.

I pluck the crown from her head and toss it on the bed as if it's a trinket, not the solid gold, sacred symbol we risked our lives for. Then, because I can't resist, I bury my hands in her soft curls. *Curls.* Who would have guessed Rapunzel had such pretty brown curls hidden beneath all that golden hair?

Aware of Wren and Quinn watching us, I grind my erection against her stomach. Tug her head forward and reclaim her lips. Force open her jaw and sweep my tongue inside, needing to get closer to her until I don't know where I end and she begins. Until my strength pours into her because I can't—*can't*—lose her again.

Good thing we're putting my brawn to good use.

As of tomorrow, I'll officially be reinstated as a knight, and I'll slide into the rank of Queen's Guard.

And speaking of sliding into things…

I pull away from Rapunzel's mouth and release her hair. Place my hands on her shoulders and walk her backward to the bed. This room, the Queen's Chamber, smells like her, yet it's foreign. Like a strange realm we must put our mark on to make it more…ours. And when I spin us around and sit on the edge of the mattress, I press down on her shoulders. Suck in a breath and exhale with a groan when she sinks to her knees between my thighs.

She creeps those deft little fingers up my thighs in a wicked tease. Behind her, Wren falls into the chair near the hearth.

Backlit by the fire, he adjusts the bulge of his crotch. Quinn, leaning against the wall, fists his cock, head tilted back as he watches us through hooded eyes. The blood rushes up my shaft, leaving me lightheaded when she grazes me with her nails.

"I've missed the taste of you." Rapunzel studies me through the thick fringe of her lashes. Licks her lips, with each undone lace of my breeches a slow torment. I want her to beg for my cock. Shove it deep down her throat until she chokes on it.

Respectfully, of course.

The large room is silent, broken by the crackle of the fire and our erratic breathing. I disrupt it with a moan when Rapunzel lays open my breeches and shoves her hand inside. She pulls me out, stroking me from base to tip. But a man can take only so much after being deprived of his woman for weeks. Still flush with the aftermath of the battle, I let my head loll back and grip her hair to guide her mouth to my aching tip.

"Prove it. Show us how much you missed his taste," Wren's graveled command has Rapunzel sliding closer. Has her seeking tongue flick over the weeping slit of my cock. I press down on her head, forcing her to swallow me. "That's it, Rapunzel. Just like that. That's our good girl."

"I know you can do better, Little Captive." I press down harder.

Her mouth is too goddamn warm—and too fucking talented. Rapunzel's panting breaths fan me as she bobs up and down my shaft. Then she drags up to the tip, licking her way around, tormenting me. The glide of her tongue against the underside of my cock has me damn near shooting right off the bed. I adjust my hold on her curls. Mutter curses. Promise to do the most wonderfully indecent things to our queen's body.

Suddenly, it's too hot here, and I tug off my shirt. Rapunzel scores my chest with her nails. Her rough touch nearly has me exploding down her throat. Through sheer force of will—thank you, years of battle training—I maintain tight control over myself. Even when she settles her eager hands on my thighs, her fingers kneading my fevered flesh.

Across the room, Quinn has his massive prick out, stroking himself. Those demon eyes are locked on Rapunzel, tracking each rise and fall of her head as she sucks me. But Wren... he's the one who likes to watch.

Not tonight, though. It's been too long.

For all of us.

Our frenetic energy sizzles throughout the room as he pulls off his boots. Then he's out of the chair and stalking across the room as he unlaces his breeches. He kicks them aside and settles behind Rapunzel. Pulls his shirt over his head and tosses it to the floor. The smattering of scars tells the story of Wren's life, of the punishments he faced when he rebelled against John. Of his hard-won freedom when he bribed, fought, and clawed his way out of Newkirk's dungeon while he still had friends within this castle. Back before John completely lost himself to his madness. Those dark times won't be forgotten, but they suddenly seem so far.

It all seems so distant, like a terrible dream fading under the gentle touch of a woman with the ferocious heart of a lion.

My womb clenches with expectation at the bite of Wren's fingers into the flesh of my thighs. I suck hard on Dax's cock, humming out a moan around his shaft when Wren slowly, gently pushes his way inside me. Stretching me. Filling me. A homecoming after too long without my men. His groan whispers behind me when he sinks in fully. Dax's hiss from the vibration of pleasure that creeps up my throat adds to the soft resonance throughout the room.

I expect to feel the brutal force of Wren's thrust. Instead, he trails his fingers down my spine to rest one hand on the small of my back. With his other, he grips my hip. Each thrust measured and deep as I bob on Dax's cock, matching Wren's steady tempo.

Wren glides his hands around from my back to my ribs. He cups my breasts. Hardens my nipples with a rough squeeze that pulls throaty moans from me. Dax's grip on my hair tightens, and he lifts his hips to thrust into my mouth, pushing himself so deep tears wet my eyes.

Wren keeps up a languid pace, loving me. Whispering sweet words. Making promises to me that tonight is only the beginning of a lifetime in his arms. *Their* arms. But with each powerful push of his hips, the friction builds. His strokes quicken. Until we burn from the pleasure raging between us.

He pulls out of me and rasps, "Get on the bed and spread your legs."

I slide my mouth off of Dax, relishing the flush on his face and the way he's watching me as I climb onto the mattress. Three sets of eyes track me as I crawl to the head of the bed. Once there, I flip onto my back and rest my weight on my elbows. To tease them, I drag my legs slowly open to draw this out.

Very slowly.

I'm not in a rush tonight.

"I can smell her desire from here," Quinn growls. "Fuck, it's so goddamn good."

"Then come closer and taste what you do to me."

Quinn's dark grin works its way right to my center, soaking me with a fresh wave of desire. "Wren needs to finish what he started." He grabs his cock and squeezes hard enough to make himself wince and groan. "You and I... I have plans for us."

Oh, God.

His raw passion speaks of all the depraved promises my body carves.

Wren crawls up the mattress and grabs my ankles. He forces my legs open wider. As wide as they can comfortably go. Wide enough to fit his broad shoulders in the space he created. Wide enough for Quinn to see him lower his head to my cunt and fuck me with his tongue. Watch as he licks me until I'm writhing against the mattress, one hand fisted in the blanket and the other in his hair. As I gasp out Wren's name, Dax traces his thumb along my lower lip. He kisses me, swallowing my next cry when Wren sucks my clit.

With Wren working my cunt, Dax pinches and pulls, then

soothes my nipples. Their collective touch creates a storm of crimson energy that swirls around me. A frenzy builds with each lash of Wren's tongue and rub of Dax's hands. Bringing me higher, and when I look at Quinn and see him watching, a wicked grin curling his beautiful mouth, a delicious tension tightens in my belly. Stretching. Contracting. Moving down my trembling legs as I squeeze Wren's head and arch my back, seeking more.

More of his tongue.

More of Dax's fingers.

I dig my heels into the mattress and press down, pushing my cunt against Wren's lips. I feel him smile against my center, and with one more wide lick from my ass to clit, Wren calls the tide to take me. I ride my climax to the end, and only once the last shudder leaves me, Dax pulls away so Wren can climb up my body.

Wren presses his fists into the mattress on both sides of my head to brace his weight. "Rapunzel," he rasps against my lips. "I'm so sorry."

"Whatever for?"

His expression pained, Wren shakes his head slowly. His eyes never leave mine. "Everything," he breathes. "You are my heart. The moment I saw you in the tower, all I am became yours."

"Oh, God, Wren, I've loved you since I was twelve, and each day since I've loved you more."

His face softens, reminding me of the boy he was when he found me in Blythe all those years ago. Finally, though, his once-angry eyes are free of the rage and grief that tainted them. They're softer. Kinder. Warm. There's…contentment…in them now.

Wren will always be my beautiful boy.

His erection, long and thick between his legs, is hot at the juncture of my thighs. He shifts his weight. Reaches between us to grip himself and, with one gentle push, enters me. My gasp fills the quiet room as my body stretches around him. He watches me as he rocks into me. Each powerful back-curling pump of his hips brings back that tension in my belly, like a ribbon coiling in my womb.

A hand smoothing the curls from my face has Wren glancing to the right. He nods at Dax, and that ribbon in my belly...? It coils tighter, and I even get lightheaded.

"Look at me, Little Captive." Giddy with the thrill of desire, I turn my head. I reach out my arm to grab for Dax. He digs one knee into the mattress and grips the headboard. "Be a good girl and open your mouth for me."

Gladly.

I part my lips and savor the weight of his heavy cock against my tongue. He glides down to the base of his shaft, nearly choking me before pulling back out, allowing me to drag in a breath. I wrap my arm around him as he pumps his hips, driving his fat cock back down my throat again and again as Wren rocks into my cunt. Across the room, watching us, Quinn growls, and the rumble inches me closer to another tidal wave.

"Keep it up with that tongue, and I'm going to come too soon," Dax groans.

"She looks so pretty, swallowing your cock," Wren tells him.

That only makes Dax mutter a curse and thrust faster, bringing tears to my eyes as I fight to breathe between the pump of his hips. "Fuck, Wren, why'd you say that? Goddamnit."

Thick ropes of cum erupt inside my mouth. I swallow it all. Dax shuffles backward, cupping his still-hard cock.

Wren nuzzles my neck and withdraws after the next punch of his hips until he pulls almost out of me. He pushes back in, whispering how scared he was when I cut my hair. How he can't lose me. And when his body tenses, every thick cord of muscle is wonderfully taut under my touch as he showers my face with kisses.

Then he promises to love me until the last star falls from the sky.

The ribbon unravels, and when the tide come, we ride it together.

Chapter Twenty-Five

QUINN

"**A**re you done being their good girl?"

Rapunzel lowers her head to regard me through the thick fringe of her lashes. "Are you ready to tell me your plans for us?"

"No, Rapunzel." I leave the support of the wall and stalk toward the bed. "By now, you know I'm a man of action."

Dax, who's busy tucking his cock back in breeches, snickers. "Sounds more like a threat to me. I'd run away screaming if I were you, Little Captive."

Her sweet laughter punches me in the chest. I've missed this lovely sound more than I'm willing to admit aloud. "*Should* I be afraid, Quinn? *Should* I run away screaming?"

I bury my hand in her soft hair, marveling at her strength and courage. "Your Highness, I doubt there is a fucking thing in all the world that will make you cower."

"Now that, Quinn Redgrave, is the nicest compliment you've ever given me."

Beauty fades. People can fake kindness. But courage? True fortitude comes from the heart and lasts a lifetime.

Her smile is radiant, her curls lovely. Her appearance may be different now, yet it's as if this is how she is *supposed* to look. As if the blonde was a hat meant to be shed. One I'm glad is gone despite my sheer terror at her fragile mortality.

Also, I reluctantly admit, I'll miss my indestructible sparring partner.

With a dark grin, I ask, "Do you trust me to make you feel good, Rapunzel?"

"Always."

The room crackles with energy as I climb onto the bed. Wren, naked, grabs the crown and leaves the bed. I'd fuck her while she wears it, but I'm going to give her a rough ride.

I'll knock the damn thing right off her pretty head.

Wren places the crown on the hearth's mantle. He pulls on his breeches and stays where he is, backlit by the fire, his eyes locked on Rapunzel. Dax falls into the chair, a predatory grin on his face as he watches us.

"Up, Your Majesty." I tug at her arm. "Turn around. I want to see your pretty ass in the air. Time to be my whore."

"Oh, God," she breathes.

I squeeze her neck, her pulse racing against my palm. "Not God."

"Quinn."

"Better," I praise her as she drops into position.

She's on full display for my hungry gaze. Without that golden hair getting in the way, I have an unobstructed view of the planes and valleys of her perfect body. Truly, Rapunzel is glorious to behold. A filthy, damned creature such as myself doesn't deserve this treasure. But I *am* a filthy, damn creature, and so I arrogantly take what I don't deserve.

I pull a vial of oil from my breeches' pocket and toss it on the bed before shucking my clothes. I planned ahead for this. Fuck, I've been thinking about doing this to her for so long. And then I'm on the bed behind her, admiring the smooth flesh of her ass. Appreciating the indent of her spine. Even now, on all fours, with her back slightly arched and her head bowed as she waits to find out how I mean to use her, she's the most elegant creature I've ever seen.

Regal.

Mine.

"Who do you belong to?"

"Rygard."

Stubborn wench, I can hear the insolence in her tone.

I give her lovely ass a sound smack. "Try again."

"You," she gasps. "I belong to you. Quinn Redgrave."

I rub the sting away. Then smack her again. "Who else?"

"Dax Stafford."

"Good girl." Another smack. This time, my palm lands on the other cheek. "And?"

Rapunzel looks right at Wren. "Wren Kincaid."

"Perfect." I kiss everywhere my palm landed on her ass. Then I snatch up the vial. Pop open the cork and spill the slippery liquid down her crack. At her hiss and clench, I soothe her. "Go easy, Princess." I use the name I always called her, even though it no longer fits her status. To me, though, she'll always be Princess. "You trust me."

She nodded. "I do."

"That's good." I re-cork the vial and toss it on the bed. "Let me make you feel good."

I massage in the oil, working it into her tight hole. She stiffens when I slide in the tip of my index finger, but I coax her back into a relaxed state. I ease it in deeper to the next knuckle. Then farther still. Slowly drive it in and out, loosening her so I can add my middle finger.

Rapunzel sucks in a hard breath and tries to crawl away, but Wren is there, his forehead against the side of her head. He whispers sweet words to her. Tender words I can never say that work to calm her.

"Ready for more, Rapunzel?"

Afraid, she shakes her head at me in answer. Wren motions for Dax. With his help, they tease her body back to life. Wren with his words. Dax fucking her cunt with his fingers. Her every breathy moan goes right to my rock-hard cock, tormenting me as I wait to slide into her.

A sheen of sweat coats me. My breathing is labored from the effort of biting back my raging desire. I almost roar my relief when Dax says, "She's soaked, Quinn."

I grip Rapunzel's hip with one hand and, with the other, take hold of the base of my cock. With gritted teeth and my breath hitched, I guide myself to the opening of her ass. "Relax, Rapunzel."

Ironically, every muscle in my body is strained so tight they're on the verge of snapping one by one.

A controlled push of my hips opens her. Another gentle drive slides in the tip, and it's so fucking beautiful the way she opens for me. I steal another inch. The oil eases my way past the band of resisting muscle. "Is she good?"

Before Dax or Wren can answer, Rapunzel tilts her head and says over her shoulder, "More. Please, oh, God, Quinn, more."

My brave warrior-queen.

She wriggles her ass and clenches her muscles. They squeeze me, pulling me in deeper. Rip a groan from me as I surge forward. Not too deep. Not too fast. Slow. Steady. I want her to want this. To beg me for my whole cock.

Her back digs with a shudder from whatever Dax is doing to her pretty cunt, and the filthy words Wren whispers in her ear. Everything primal inside me works its way through the cracks. Turning me practically feral. My guttural moan fills the room as I claim more of her. Rapunzel meets my next thrust, pushing back against me. Until I'm halfway in, and she's grasping the hand Dax has buried inside her. Shoving him deeper. Grinding his fingers against my cock, he and I separated only by the thin barrier of her warm, wet inner wall. She leans toward Wren, rambling incoherent answers to his filthy promises.

I grip her other hip. Dig in my stance. One more rock forward fully seats me inside her. Wren grabs her jaw and turns her head to capture her mouth. Her cry tumbles down his throat as I withdraw…

…then sink back inside her.

Again and again.

Claiming her gorgeous ass as my own.

I fuck Rapunzel in a frenzy. Lose myself in the tight squeeze of her ass around my cock as her climax builds. "That's it, Princess. Come for me."

Sparks ignite behind my eyes as pleasure builds at the base of my spine.

Quickening my pace and deepening each stroke, that pleasure grows to a painful pressure that whips around to my balls in glorious torment that travels up my shaft. And then Rapunzel stiffens, her limbs locking, her breaths coming in shallow gasps. Dax keeps working her as Wren digs a hand in her hair and gives it a soft tug that sets her on a precipice.

"You're with us, Rapunzel," he whispers. "You're safe. Jump, Zee. We'll catch you."

And, oh fuck, she does.

Rapunzel leaps, riding my cock with beautiful, wild abandon as her orgasm sends her off a cliff. She takes me with her, and together we dive into a raging sea as I empty myself inside her.

It is a…homecoming.

I always hated Newkirk.

Too drafty. Mostly, though, it was always full of John's rot and ruin. When I sent him to Hell, he took his evil with him.

I'll meet him there one day and have my fun with him, but that's a long way off. I want a whole life to live with Rapunzel.

A *long* fucking life.

That's not asking too much, and as I trace between Rapunzel's shoulder blades, an odd…contentment settles over me. I silently beg a god I hope is listening to allow me to die an old man, warm in my bed, surrounded by these people.

My family.

At The Cup and Crown, Rapunzel told Sir Walter she was weary of all this death.

I understand what she meant now.

Everyone I swore to kill is now dead. I avenged my family. Rapunzel is queen. I want to live peacefully before I spend eternity in Hell.

With Rygard's lovely queen sprawled across my chest, I know she's awake despite her eyes being closed. We're all wide awake, holding on to these last few hours before the world intrudes.

Dax is back on the chair by the hearth, watching the flames. Wren sits beside us on the bed, tucked under the blanket. He hasn't taken his eyes off Rapunzel.

Our exquisite little queen props herself up on her elbow with her chin supported on her upturned palm. "You're tense. Why?" I shrug one shoulder. "Quinn Redgrave, this is a good night. We won. Tell me why there is tension in your gorgeous body."

I am not a man given to blushing, yet my face heats at her compliment. "You died tonight."

"No, I almost died. There is a difference," Rapunzel counters. "I had a plan and executed it to perfection."

I lift a brow at that. "Your plan was reckless and left you mortal." I twirl one of her short curls around my finger. "Pray tell us, Princess, what was going through this pretty head when you sheared off the rest of your hair?"

She has the audacity to heave out a sigh as if she's about to issue the simplest of explanations to the simplest of minds. "Half of the blonde was already gone. How would you have treated me from this day forward, knowing half my life was gone?" I go to speak but snap my jaw shut. Thin my lips to a defeated line because any answer I give her will justify her actions. "Exactly," she says, filling my disgruntled silence.

"So you attempted to kill yourself so we wouldn't fuss over you?" Dax says, his voice sleepy but holding a note of frustration. "Hate to point out the obvious, Little Captive, but if having half a head of magic hair would have us fretting over you, imagine how we're going to worry over you now that you're breakable."

She rolls her eyes and sits up, dragging the blanket to cover her perfect breasts. "The three of you would have treated each strand like it was precious."

"Because they *were* precious," I growl.

"They kept you alive," Wren adds.

Her exasperated glare travels across us. "I spent my life in a physical cage. The prospect of living the rest of it in an invisible one was unbearable."

"So unbearable you risked death?"

"Yes," Rapunzel answers Wren without a hint of hesitation or guilt. "Victory at any cost and freedom at any price. Remember?"

Wren trails his knuckles down her cheek. "I remember, Zee."

She tilts her head to lean into his touch. "Besides," she adds with a drowsy grin. "I knew I was safe. The three of you wouldn't let me die."

Her confidence in us humbles me, and I am not a man easily made vulnerable. But here I am, flayed open right down to my bare nerves. Exposed. Raw. Especially when she turns away from Wren and places her little hand on my cheek.

I bite down hard on my lip to hold back words that leap onto my tongue, Words I don't dare speak because…because despite her tender touch and sweet declarations, it can't erase what I've done—the bargain I made.

Where I'm bound once this life is over.

Rapunzel frowns when her gaze falls on my lip. "You're bleeding."

I lick away the salty tang. "I can't."

The divot between her brows deepens. "Can't what, Quinn?"

I shake my head. "Rapunzel…"

She sits up and buried her hands in the mess of my hair. "Quinn, talk to me."

"Fucking fine." Suddenly, I'm keenly aware of the weight of Wren and Dax's stares. How they're able to hear what I'm about to confess. And yet, I need to say this to her because tonight, we nearly lost her, which changed everything. We *all* could have died, and she would have never known how important she is to me. "I may not be a man of many words like Dax or pretty ones like Wren, but it is a truth, Rapunzel, that I love you."

There.

The truth.

I love this woman. Love her so fucking much, and when I lick away the remaining blood from my lips, Rapunzel's captivating green eyes go wide as my tongue disappears back inside my mouth. Then a choked gasp whispers from her as an unseen entity tosses her from the bed. Wren tumbles after her as if shoved off the mattress. Dax is out of the chair and diving for his sword that's somewhere discarded on the floor.

And me…

Oh, my fucking God.

Agony tears through me, stealing the breath right out of me. I gape, furious…yes, even terrified….at the shadowy figure that emerges like smoke across the room. My first instinct is to protect. Protect Rapunzel. Protect Wren and Dax. But I can't fucking move as that massive gray body shuffles toward the bed. Ominous. Bringing with it the acrid stink of Hell. The demon tilts its head, regarding me with those onyx eyes, and all I can think is, *'No, not now. Not yet. And not while I'm sitting here naked.'*

How undignified.

This prick could have at least given me the honor of dying with my sword in my hand—and with breeches covering my bare ass.

"Couldn't wait, could you? Couldn't let me be fucking happy," I grind out, every part of me but my mouth locked in place by the demon. "You had to kill me right when I was finally fucking happy."

The demon laughs in my face.

I scan the room and catch sight of Wren and Dax shielding Rapunzel on the far side of the chamber. At least someone thought to give her Wren's shirt to cover her nudity. My only solace is that the demon will spare them. The beast is here for me, not them. Once it takes my soul, it will leave them unharmed. Why? Because a deal is a deal. I'm the only one who owes this creature a damn thing.

Literally.

My damned soul.

"If you think I'm going to make it easy for you to torture me, you're as foolish as you are grotesque."

"Temper, temper, Quinn Redgrave." The demon calmly *tsks* me, its cloven feet banging against the stone as it paces a U-shape around the bed. "It seems I've no need of your putrid soul."

"You lie," I growl.

The demon ceases its pacing and cuts me a glare. "I may not be above trickery, but I am no liar." It shifts its hellish gaze to Rapunzel, and my blood runs cold. "Isn't that true, Queen Rapunzel? Am I not honoring our bargain?"

"What?" My roar rebounds off the stone walls as the

appalling image of Rapunzel being torn to shreds in Hell flashes through my mind. "Rapunzel, what did you do?"

Rapunzel shrinks back, but not even Wren and Dax can protect her. With a wave of its hand, the demon shoves them away without physically touching them. "Two truths to redeem his soul for a single strand of my hair. That's what was promised, and that's what was given."

The demon stomps to the side of the bed. Leans toward me, close enough that the sulfur on its breath gags me. In a conspiratorial gesture, it holds a clawed finger to its lips. "It was our secret, Queen Rapunzel and mine." It lowers its hand and braces itself on the mattress, its weight pulling me closer still. "If she whispered a word of our bargain, the pact was broken." Then it sniffs me and grimaces as if I'm the one who *stinks*. "Truth is, Quinn Redgrave, I would have released your toxic soul even had she reneged on our agreement."

Without warning or ceremony, the demon clamps a hand around my throat and squeezes. Don't know how its grip doesn't crush my neck. Gasping, I open my mouth and fight for my next breath, which allows the demon to press its disgusting mouth to mine.

The demon exhales.

I cough.

It growls and exhales again. The vile taste of its revolting salvia makes drips down my throat. Noble-born and warrior-bred, I have the instinct to fight. To feel the comforting weight of my sword in my hand. The warm spray of my enemy's blood on my flesh marked me as the victor of the battle. Instead, all I can do is sit there, my back pinned to the wall and my ass to the bed as the demon breathes into me.

Filling me…

Filling me with my soul.

Oh, God, please let this be real. Don't let me be dead, and this be naught but a cruel, hellish torment.

When the demon pulls away and spits on the floor, it whips around to face Rapunzel. Bows its head. "Our bargain is complete, Queen Rapunzel. May you all rot in Heaven."

And then it drops back into the shadows, and my body becomes my own. Rapunzel races across the room and throws herself at me. "Talk to me, Quinn. Please. Are you—"

"I feel it." I place my hand—*my flesh-colored hand*—on my non-marked chest, the hammer of my heartbeat strong against my palm. "Rapunzel…" I grab her hand and replace mine with hers. "Here. Touch me. I'm whole again."

"Yes, Quinn, you are." She's crying, nodding. "Oh, God, your eyes are blue."

"Here." Dax shoves a goblet at me. "Get the taste of that fucking creature out of your mouth."

I accept the metal goblet and gulp down a long swallow of the spiced wine. It tastes…different. Better. Richer. Delicious. "Christ. That was… Remind me never to do anything that stupid again." Then to Rapunzel, "Why would you summon it?"

"I would never." Appalled at the accusation, she glares down her little imperial nose at me. "*It* came to *me*. It said you lost your appeal and that once you regain your soul, you'll be my problem."

Sorry, but I have to laugh at that despite how this night keeps getting stranger and stranger. "Problem?"

"Seems you have a wild soul," she drawls.

I haul Rapunzel onto my lap. "It may be wild, but at least it's finally mine again."

"Try not to be reckless with it in the future," Wren warns me as he slides into the bed beside us.

"Never again." I kiss Rapunzel. "Too much at stake now."

"Move the fuck over. I'm tired." Dax shoves Wren closer to Rapunzel. "In case you forgot, we killed a king and usurped his kingdom. I don't know about you, but I'd like to get at least an hour or two of sleep before we wake up."

Ignoring her yelp, Dax repositions Rapunzel. He yanks off the blanket. Shakes it out and lays it atop us before crawling up on the large mattress and tucking himself beside us. Still, it's cramped with our three large bodies crowding Rapunzel, but I'll bet my sword arm not one of us will leave this bed tonight.

As I drift off to sleep with Rapunzel in my arms, I have love and hope in my soul for the first time in over two years.

I am a happy man.

Once upon a time, Blithe Forest was cursed.

A witch lived here, hidden among the ancient trees and twisted, thorny foliage. Most folks didn't dare venture too far south of Leeds Village once they crossed the Merrie River. Scared, the lot of them, they were. But not me. My father always said I was fearless. My mother called me reckless. I remember asking myself how anyone could be afraid on such a fine day when the sun filtered through the canopy of trees and made the pollen sparkle like fine jewels.

Besides, if the witch tried any of her foul magic on me, I had a trusty stick as a weapon to protect me.

Little did I know, Sybil led me to the tower that day.

She led me to Rapunzel.

It had to be you. Sybil scrawled to me on a piece of parchment. Her gnarled fingers flew furiously while she recovered from her ordeal in the dungeon. Gone is her tongue, making it impossible for her to weave her spells, yet she is content. Joyous for Rapunzel's happiness. *Your parents and I knew you would protect our princess.*

It makes sense now how I could 'sneak' away to visit

Rapunzel while she was locked in the tower. My parents never asked me where I'd been, even when I was gone for hours and hours. Nor did I question how I could always find my way to and from the tower when everyone else became hopelessly lost within the enchanted forest.

Sybil always showed me the way.

But what they failed to realize was that Rapunzel never needed me. She needed no one. Not even to rescue her from the tower. That she could have done herself. All I did was give her the push she needed to walk out on her own.

She embraced her freedom and conquered a king.

All we did was help her along the way.

The stubborn woman thought to make me her king. *Never.* She is Queen, and no one shall outrank her in Rygard. Instead, I reluctantly accepted the title of Prince Consort.

Quinn took Sir Walter's place as Captain of the Guard. He now oversees the royal garrison, with the older man retired in peace and good fortune, as he deserves.

Not to be outdone, Dax is the Queen's Guard, and he takes his job too seriously. Especially when I catch him with his hand up Rapunzel's skirt to check that certain body parts are duly protected when no one else is watching.

It's been months, and word of our coup spread throughout the kingdom. A steady stream of Rygardians came to pay their respects to their new queen. Already, the tension that once gripped this land is gone. A newfound—and hard-won—tranquility has settled over this kingdom.

My parents would be proud of what we accomplished.

They would have loved Rapunzel.

I gaze across the courtyard and see Eleanor and Rygard's queen running around barefoot, playing with a handful of children. I remember when Rapunzel asked me what grass felt like. Swaddled like a newborn despite the warmth of this lovely spring afternoon, Sybil sits on a bench watching them as well.

Now and again, she smiles at the peals of laughter coming from Rapunzel, Eleanor, and the children.

"Lord Eddington made an offer for my sister's hand," Quinn says as he strolls over to me.

I roll my eyes. "That old goat?"

"Our benevolent queen left it up to me to respectfully decline his offer."

My brows shoot up as I drag my gaze from Rapunzel to Quinn. "I trust the man is still among the living?"

Although he regained his soul, Quinn kept his chilling glare. He gestures to his blue and gold tunic—Rapunzel's colors. "My days of senseless murder are over. I've got rank now."

"For fuck's sake," I scoff. "And didn't it go to your head."

"Careful, Wren," he warns. "That doesn't mean I'm not above giving you a right good beating on the lists."

Dax joins us, *tsking*. "Now, now, Quinn. Can't go beating up the *Prince Consort*." He puts a sarcastic emphasis on my title.

"He even gets to sleep in the special bed," Quinn says mockingly.

"If I recall, your naked ass was in that bed last night, not mine."

The 'special bed' being Rapunzel's.

Dax raises his hand. "Fuck off with both of you. Tomorrow is mine."

Usually, we're all together, the four of us—and tonight, we have something planned for her. Sometimes, however, we require private time with Rapunzel. It's fun to share, but it's also nice to have that intimacy with her.

"I apologize in advance if she falls asleep on us tonight." Quinn is about as far from contrite as a man can be. "Considering how…strenuous…last night was for her, she might be worn out tonight. Or it could be because the two of you are just dull."

Who would have fathomed that Quinn Redgrave has a

playful edge to him? But ever since he regained his soul, his wit came shining through.

"Kiss my ass," Dax quips.

"No, thank you," Quinn shoots back. "I'd rather kiss Rapunzel's.

"Kiss my what?"

"Your Highness," we say in unison as we bow to her. Propriety and all that in public because she is, after all, our queen. Privately, she will always be my Zee, Quinn's Princess, and Dax's Little Captive.

"Your ass," Quinn snaps.

Rapunzel gives him a little knowing grin. "I believe you did plenty of that last night."

"And I believe you enjoyed it." Quinn leans close to her, but not too close. We are always aware of watching eyes. "Plenty."

A pretty blush heats her cheeks. "Enough of that. Your sister would have a word with you, *Sir* Quinn." Rapunzel's first order of business the day after our coup was reinstating Quinn and Dax's knighthoods. She also knighted me, and while Sir Wren still sounds wrong, I'm getting used to it. "Sir Dax, please help Sybil return to the hall. She's getting chilled."

Dax scoops up Rapunzel's hand and places a kiss on her knuckles. "Anything for you, Your Highness."

Then he's off, dragging Quinn with him.

"I would have a private word with you, please," I say to her.

Still barefoot, Rapunzel hitches up her yellow gown and marches across the courtyard. I follow her into the grand stone chapel. Cardinal Bram conducts mass here, but not today. Today is special, and the magnificent church is empty. "Now that you have me alone, whatever will you do with me?"

The possibilities are endless—but not here, and not now, despite the raging need to lift her skirt and fuck her even under the watchful eye of God himself.

Sunlight filters through arched, stained-glass windows,

casting a muted rainbow of colors across the dim chapel. She scans the area, her curls swirling around her lovely face. Her hair has grown. It flows past her shoulders. The contrast of her fair skin, green eyes, and dark hair is striking.

Satisfied no one is hiding at the altar, or between the pews, she closes the distance between us, rises on her tiptoes, and kisses my lips tenderly.

"I've been aching to do that all morning," she whispers.

I press my forehead to hers. "I should be angry with you."

"Whatever for?"

"You forgot again." I stroke the back of her hair. Down her spine. "What am I going to do with you, Zee?"

"Wren," she whines, dragging out the ending of my name. "Explain, please."

I should keep her guessing, but I'm not that mean.

Pulling away from her, I dig my hand into my breeches' pocket. I extend my arm and open my hand. Rapunzel looks down. Blinks. Then gasps. She reaches out and reverently accepts a freshly picked peony.

"Happy twenty-fifth birthday, Rapunzel."

With tears spilling down her cheeks, she clutches the flower to her chest. "This is much different from the last time you gave me a peony."

"I wouldn't take back that day, even if I could."

Her watery grin cuts straight to my heart. "I rather enjoyed what you did to me against that tower." She glances at the peony, then back at me. "Thank you, Wren, for everything. For finding me, and for loving me, and for saving me. I would have died in that tower if you hadn't set me free."

I wipe the tears from her cheeks. Kiss the tip of her nose. Then I give her a slow, measured shake of my head. "No, Rapunzel, you would have been fine. I didn't free you. All I did was give you a gentle push to the door, but you walked yourself out. Don't you see that? You're the real magic. It was never your hair.

It was always *you*. Just you. Your light. Your strength. Your courage. You *are* Rygard." I take her free hand and place it on my chest. "You are the beating heart of this kingdom. Our heart." I curl my fingers around hers and tug her toward the door. "Now, let's go celebrate your birthday properly."

"It's been decades since Newkirk lit the lanterns."

A deep divot appears between Rapunzel's brows as we stand with her on the Great Balcony. We purposely brought her up here for the unobstructed view of the south garden. The sun finally finished its descent below the horizon. Even the weather knows how important tonight's surprise is for Rygard's queen.

After all, every member of her staff assembled to light up the night sky for her.

"Lanterns?"

"You'll see," Little Captive," Dax says softly from beside her.

"This is all for you. They love you." Behind her, Quinn runs a hand down her spine. "We love you."

Although I'm the only one who can openly show Rapunzel public affection—I am her Prince Consort, out of respect for Quinn and Dax, I refrain. I do, however, grab her hand and give it a gentle squeeze. "They've planned this for weeks."

Below us, one by one, Newkirk's staff lights the rectangular lanterns they spent so much time making for tonight. For their queen, who saved them from a tyrant.

To be with her on this special occasion—the first time she's ever celebrating her birthday.

And one by one, those lanterns lift into the air, floating over our heads. But I don't watch them. I don't even *see* them. All I see is Rapunzel. Rapunzel, once watched the world from a single window and dreamed of a life beyond the tower. Now, she's

Queen of Rygard, reaching out to touch the lights as they drift over her head.

Lights that are beacons of hope for a healing kingdom.

A hope made possible because of a tiny woman who possesses the courage of the mightiest of souls.

This one took a motherfucking village.

Frankie: "Go write," are the sweetest words you say to me. They keep my ass in the chair and my mind on the characters. Without you, I would still be that person who dreamed of one day, maybe, perhaps, writing a book. I love you so much, Chest Brockwell. (heh)

Jesse and Tyler: Thank you for cheering me on despite (many) pizza dinners while I struggled to get to the end of this story. I love you both with everything I am.

Becca: Thank you for encouraging me to keep going and to drown out the negativity when that noise became a roar. You know how close I came to giving up on this one. Rapunzel owes you. *Big time*. Thank you for bringing it together. I adore you.

Charly: Okay, but yes, you encouraged me to get to the end of this book, but now it's my turn to grab the pompoms and cheer for you! I'm so proud of you and can't wait to devour your first book. Go little rockstar! Love you!

Lina: I doubt you'll ever realize how much your friendship means to me, but there are many times I kept writing because you believe in me. I absolutely treasure you.

Allister: I'm so grateful you took a chance on *Twisted*— because now I can openly stalk you. Heh No, but seriously. I LOVE the videos you send me. You have no idea how many times I was in a funk and the notification came that you shared a video with me and it made my morning better.

Chrishawn: My gawd, woman. It was touch and go there, wasn't it? Thank you for holding my hand right up to the finish line. Those last few voices messages… LOL They saved my sanity.

Sarah: My silly, lovely, beautiful, AWESOME sweetheart. I'm so glad the Tok brought us together. You make me laugh every time we talk—so, like every damn day. The Mad Hatter is going to love you.

Patrons: Thank you for supporting me, even when I go quiet because my broken brain can't do two things at once. I do hope you enjoyed the previews I shared of *Twined*, and I can't wait to start dropping fun snippets from *Shattered*. Love you all so much!

My (incredible) Readers: Holy shit, I l adore the breath right out of you. When I started Twisted, I never imagined so many people would come along with me on Rapunzel's journey. But you did, and I thank you so much because without you, I would have surely given up on her. Getting to the end of this book wasn't easy. I fought for every word, but every time I wanted to throw int he towel, I'd hop on TikTok or Instagram and find messages of love for these characters. I couldn't let you down. I had to fight through to the end and give Rapunzel—*and you*—this Happily Ever After.

About the Author

Renee Rocco loves to lose herself in dark romances. She writes complex, damaged antiheroes, pairing them with beautifully tormented heroines. Although she jumps Romance genres, switching between Contemporary to Dark Fantasy, she got her start in Paranormal. She shamelessly abuses the em dash and ellipsis, and is addicted to bubble tea. By day, Renee works for a NY publisher, with her nights spent indulging in her imagination. Beneath the glamour of work-from-home mom duties, she's a suburban misfit who always has a sarcastic comment at the ready—whether the situation calls for one or not. She's not Instagram-ready or speakerphone-friendly (you've been warned).

Sign up for Renee's newsletter and be the first to receive news and exclusive previews. Or join her on Patreon where she's sharing her out-of-print series, the Templar vampires, extended previews of upcoming books, plus so much more!
https://reneerocco.com

instagram.com/reneeroccoauthor

patreon.com/reneerocco

tiktok.com/@reneeroccoauthor

amazon.com/Renee-Rocco/e/B01LLT5VXE

pinterest.com/reneeroccoauthor

facebook.com/reneeroccoauthor

Forget what you've read.
There is no Prince Charming in this fairy tale.

Rapunzel spent her life as a willing prisoner locked inside a tower. Protected by magic and guarded by a witch, she believed Happily Ever Afters are the stuff of fables…

Read where it all began!
https://reneerocco.com/twisted

Prologue

ERIC

Post–Civil War II
Mayhem, Pennsylvania

"Hi."

I resist the urge to grin when I look up from the textbook resting on my lap. Shielding my eyes against the afternoon sun, I see Jamie Ellis hovering over me. My pulse quickens, and my palms go slick, but she can't know I'm excited. I'm friggin' thrilled, but I'm Eric Shaw, and I have a reputation to uphold. "Why'd you miss school yesterday?"

She shrugs and squats beside me. Adjusts the skirt of her ugly blue dress around bruised legs. The clean scents of soap and shampoo cling to her. "Whatcha reading?"

Most people avoid me. Not Jamie. She's a tiny warrior invading my space. I don't mind, though. We've known each other since kindergarten, but from a distance. Things changed late last semester. I caught Kyle McCarter groping her in the hallway and beat the living shit out of him. When the new school year started, Jamie glued herself to my side. For the last nine months, we've spent every lunch period together.

Not going to lie. This girl being in my shadow annoyed the hell out of me at first, but I didn't want to hurt her feelings. I mean, hell, everyone knows she gets beat by her dad. Saw no reason to be a dick to her. Figured she'd go back to keeping to herself. She didn't, and then she grew on me, like mold. My friends accepted her because they knew I'd kick their asses if they didn't.

Now, weekends suck because she can't hang out. Her asshole father locks her up in their house over on Vine Street, only letting her out to go to school and the library.

The thing is, Jamie got dealt a raw deal, and nobody seems to want to do a damn thing about it. But *someone* has to have her back. Standing at over six feet tall and muscular to balance out the height, I'm a big kid. Appointed myself her unofficial body-guard. At school, anyway. Can't help her when she's at home.

Not yet, anyway.

But I'm working on a plan.

Tiny details about her get me going, and I have to remind myself Jamie's not my girlfriend. Doesn't stop me from wanting her. Can't help it. When you get past the thrift store from hell wardrobe, she's friggin' gorgeous. And other guys see it, too, but they know they have to go through me to get to her and that's not happening.

They're horny, not suicidal.

Can't blame them for trying, though. She's got the cutest sprinkling of freckles on the bridge of her nose. Her green eyes are speckled with what looks like golden glitter. Her face is flaw-less skin and sharp angles, giving her an almost mythical appear-ance. Like some fairy-tale creature come to life. Hard to tell if the body buried beneath the ugly, oversized dresses has curves or not, but I'm going to go with no. Personally, I don't give a shit. She's perfect as far as I'm concerned.

What I do notice is that when she's nervous, Jamie wrings her hands until the skin's splotchy, and she scrunches her face into an adorable scowl when she's pissed. And there's the bruises everyone pretends not to see—myself included. She doesn't talk about them, *ever*. Most times, it's like I'm the one person who gives a shit if she's hungry and hurting. I mean, yeah, I can beat the hell out of all the Kyle McCarters in the whole damn world, but I can't do for her what an adult can.

I can't save her from her dad.

But everything changes in two years.

Jamie has to hold on a little longer. Once we're eighteen, I'm getting her away from her father so she can start a life for herself.

I tap the tip of her nose. "A book is what I'm reading, Runt."

Jamie scoots closer until our thighs touch. Her heat seeps through the denim of my jeans, sending a rush of blood to my dick. Because, yeah, what I need right now is a hard-on in the middle of the schoolyard. *Outstanding.* Her hand shakes as she tucks a lock of her shoulder-length hair behind her ear. She tilts her face to the sky, her expression, as always, unreadable. "On sunny days, I can imagine being someplace else. Somewhere clean."

Her head's angle shows a fresh burn the size of a cigarette on her neck, below her ear.

Sonofabitch.

Jamie squeezes her eyes shut, and I give her a quick once-over to see if the bastard did more damage. There's a new, fist-sized mark on her chin. Lip's got a small split, too. My gut tells me if her father keeps this up, he's going to kill her before I have the chance to get her away from him. Then I'll have to kill him, and it'll be a colossal mess.

Maybe it's time my father teaches Billy Ellis what happens to a grown-ass man who uses his daughter as a punching bag.

"I love Mayhem," I remind her for the billionth time.

Jamie opens her eyes and gapes at me for a full thirty

seconds before laughing in my face. It's the first time I've heard her laugh—truly laugh—since I've known her.

"Impossible."

"It's true," I counter.

Mayhem is in my blood. My dad's Unholy, and at sixteen, I'm already on my way to following in his footsteps. I'm positive my best friend, Luke Hayden, and I are why Sheriff Warren is a raving drunk with a nervous tic.

"Yes, well, you would. You're Mayhem royalty." She plucks the history textbook off of my legs. "Light reading?"

I shrug. "Finals are next week."

Rusty Shaw is big on school and made me promise I'd graduate. Since I have to be here anyway, I figure I might as well do my dad one better and finish with honors.

If anyone other than Jamie or Luke saw me reading the book, I'd make a joke rather than admit to studying. With her, I don't have to be that guy. My so-called bad-boy reputation doesn't impress her.

She examines the photos of old America splashed across the textbook's glossy page. "Must be nice to be the smartest kid in class."

I work my ass off to get good grades. Hence, studying while I waited for Jamie to walk her cute butt over to me.

"Knowledge is power." I've adopted my dad's motto.

"True." She turns the page and taps the photo of a lit-up and bustling Times Square. "Ever wonder what the world was like before the war?"

"Never."

According to history, the conflict began on social media at the same time a global pandemic killed off a shitload of the world's population. Online mobs created a nanny state that decimated fundamental freedoms. The fighting spilled over into the physical world. Riots erupted. Bloodbaths sparked a Second Civil War. Millions were slaughtered, and America burned.

When the battle ended, a fractured nation emerged from the ashes with no real winner and only degrees of loss.

We're still cleaning up the mess, with huge chunks of the country buried under rubble and trapped in chaos.

Jamie sets the book aside and steeples her legs. When she rests her chin on her knees, I get a peek at the black shorts beneath her skirt—and the bruising on her inner thighs.

Christ, no.

My jaw clenches and my muscles stiffen as fury turns my blood to lava. I'm about to ask Jamie the brutal question, already plotting how I'm going to kill Ellis and dispose of his body, when she stops me dead with an announcement that cools my rage and replaces it with dread.

"I'm going away."

No one strays far from Mayhem. The town has its own gravity, grounding everyone who lives here.

I hide my skepticism. Or is it fear? *Whatever.* "Yeah? Where are you going?"

"Someplace I'll hate more than Mayhem."

I want to put my arms around her, but I don't, afraid I'll spook her. Jamie hates being touched. Can't say I blame her. "Stay. Problem solved."

"Can't." She stretches out her legs. There are more marks on her shins. "I came to school to say goodbye and to thank you for being my friend."

Jamie pops onto her knees and faces me. I stay as still as death when she grips my shoulders. I may not be relationship material, but I would be better for her. *Only* for her. Then she surprises the hell out of me by leaning in real close to press her mouth to mine.

I lick the taste of apples off her lips.

As of this second, apples are my favorite fruit.

When Jamie moves away, I'm tempted to haul her back for another kiss. But I don't because teachers are watching, and when she glances over her shoulder, I track her gaze to the squad car parked outside the schoolyard. Her sad smile is a knife in my heart. She stands and brushes dirt off her bare knees. Then she spins on the heel of her scuffed, white Vans, and before I can stop her, she marches toward the school. I should chase after her. Instead, like an asshole, I stay stuck to the spot beneath the tree and watch as she disappears inside the old, brick building.

Time grinds to a halt, but somehow, the minutes still fly by.

Five...

Ten...

The bell rings, marking the end of the lunch period. I grab the textbook and join the student lineup, taking a place behind Luke. He had a growth spurt this year and finally caught up to my height.

"What's the sheriff doing here?" Luke asks over his shoulder.

"No clue," I say, but I have a sick feeling it has everything to do with Jamie.

As we shuffle toward the entrance, Sheriff Warren comes marching out. He's not alone. I don't know what shocks me more —Jamie's kiss lingering on my lips or seeing her led away in handcuffs.

Chapter 1

WRAITH

Eight Years Later
Marion County, Florida

I'm positive of one absolute truth—I'm not dying in this cage.

Bad enough, David Crane makes bank off my fights. I won't give him the satisfaction of profiting from my death.

It's Fight Night, and the Coliseum's ground floor is packed. Rows of chairs ten deep wrap around a steel cage in the center of the prestigious arena. A cloud of tobacco smoke thickens air rank with too much cologne, perfume, and sweat. Strategically placed bouncers serve as crowd control. Provocative, leather-clad bartenders hustle to keep pace with the steady flow of orders. Flirtatious waitresses work an upscale horde, sating the mob's appetite for liquor while fighters quench their thirst for violence.

The action flows to a brothel above the arena. Up there, enough money buys limitless debauchery. Shit those sick fucks do in the luxury rooms is so bad, we won't even allow it in Mayhem—and our motto is *Pick your pleasure*, so…

Yeah. It's fucking disgusting.

Crane built himself a kingdom on the border of Ocala

National Forest. As far as I know, there's only one way in or out, making Gomorrah virtually inescapable. But trust I'm getting out of here, and it won't be in a body bag.

Never turn your back on your enemy.

The warning echoes in my head. Keeps me upright long after I should have fallen. My opponent is taller than me, agile, too, but slim. Felix's jabs are quick, but I'm quicker. His kicks brutal, but I'm stronger. The guy has landed more than a few solid hits, and I swear he's ruptured something vital when he roundhouses me. But I'm a brick shithouse and I withstand the battering, giving better than I receive.

Shame I have to kill him. He's putting up a hell of a fight.

Cracked ribs are razor blades grating against my lungs. Sweat stings my eyes. My brain is bashed around inside my skull, with each crash of Felix's fist doing more damage. But I'm still alive.

Mayhem born and raised, I've fought my way to the top of the Unholy's food chain, earning a place as the gang's most feared enforcer. I know how to hurt someone, and I dig deep as I swing my right arm in a heavy overhand, aiming for an imaginary target beyond Felix's head. The goal is never to hit the person. It's to punch *through* them. I aim past him, the slam of my knuckles shattering flesh and bone. Christ, I destroy the man's face, ruining his orbital socket.

I'm relentless. Can't give Felix a shred of mercy. Instead, I bare my teeth, an animal moving in for the kill, and hammer him with a volley of punches until my arms scream from exhaustion.

Concussed, I see three of Felix and maintain the attack on the one in the middle. He crawls away, groping at the mat, and gains his feet. I spit out a mouthful of blood and charge forward. I nail him hard enough to buckle his legs. My guard stays up, and although I never hesitate, I'm still a fucking human being beneath this…monster…and I can't bring myself to whale on a man when he's on his knees.

Die, damn you.

There's no glory in my inevitable victory—no honor in beating someone who lost the fight a dozen punches ago. But the battle won't end until one of us is dead.

The crowd's roar is thunderous, their bloodlust sickening. These people are supposed to be civilized members of society. God-fearing, law-abiding aristocracy who glare down their collective nose at folks who live outside of their manicured world. To them, I'm trash—less than nothing. A criminal who, they believe, has earned my place in this cage.

Screw them.

Felix pushes to his feet, his legs unsteady. He doesn't raise his arms. He's not protecting himself, and he's not putting up a fight. A ghost of a grin lifts his bleeding lips. Holy shit, the guy is gone. Checked out. The battering trashed his brain. Completely busted him to hell. It's no consolation to my conscience, but he knew he would die tonight. I saw the defeat in his eyes when he entered the cage. Saw his fear—and ultimately his acceptance—when the door locked behind us. It's a surrender I'd seen on other fighters when they knew they'd lost before the battle began. Doesn't make having to kill this man any easier.

Nor was it easy for me to end the seven opponents who came before him.

Felix's face will make eight I'll never unsee.

Eight men whose blood will slowly drown me until I'm dead.

But not today.

As Crane's current champion, I've become the perfect killing machine. The reigning fan favorite. The main attraction who draws a prestigious crowd. Shit, even Marion County's mayor turned out for tonight's event. Corrupt prick was waiting for me when the handlers brought me up from the dungeon. Claimed he wanted to meet me. *Bullshit.* His actual motive was to warn me that I better win because he has a fortune riding on my match.

Politicians. Gotta love the worthless douchebags.

I raise my arm to deliver the killing blow that will put a shit-load of money in Mayor Dickhead's pocket.

The mob chants the name Crane gave me, and it makes my skin crawl.

Atticus. Atticus. Atticus.

The noise disorients me as I tower over Felix. With my fist hovering in midair, I pause. Waiting… Felix gives me a barely perceptible nod. A silent plea to end his agony. The steel links of the octagon close in on me. My heart hammers a punishing beat. I lick chapped lips and taste Felix's defeat mingled with the coppery tang of blood.

I'm fucking sorry, man.

This isn't me.

You sure?

I silence the voice screaming in my head, content with the knowledge that I've never murdered an innocent man until I was brought to Gomorrah and forced into the cage.

Two hundred twenty pounds drives my fist. The punch nails Felix square in the temple. The unstoppable force colliding with a solid object that cracks his skull. Felix's head snaps to the side. His torso twists at the waist. He hangs there, suspended, then tips forward. He hits the mat with a heavy thud.

He twitches.

His body stills.

Blood pools under his head.

Fight's over.

Rage and regret collide when I spin to face Crane. The object of my fury sits front row with his slicked-back blond hair and expensive gray suit. A false idol among mortals. I gnash my teeth and snarl at the crowd, giving them the animal they demand. Politicians and law enforcement pepper the crush of bodies. Greedy bastards are on Crane's payroll, relishing the violence as they applaud my ignoble victory.

I may be the weapon, but the crowd crammed inside the Coliseum are equally responsible for Felix's death.

I'm about to turn away, the sight of them repulsive, but a face catches my attention. The world tunnels, and all I see is *her*, sitting beside Crane with an expression as blank as Felix's. She's an understated spectacle in a white dress among the garish mob. A cloud of wavy brown hair tumbles over her shoulders. Angular features remind me of a grown version of someone I forced myself to forget. Someone I can't afford to remember. Not here, because she's my one weakness, and if there's one thing I can't be in Gomorrah, it's vulnerable.

With hands clasped on her lap, the woman watches me, and I swear she can see straight to my fucking soul. Right down to the filth festering inside me. To the monster clawing at my skull, fighting to break free. But there's no judgment in her striking eyes. Those eyes that weave a spell and, bizarrely, calms the rage sizzling through my veins.

Maybe Felix isn't the only man who died in the cage. Maybe she's an angel come to usher me out of this hell.

Nah. I'm in too much pain to be dead.

And I'm sure as shit not bound for heaven.

I earned a place in hell on my eighteenth birthday. The day I became an Unholy.

Spell's broken. I tear my gaze from her and swipe my arm across my eyes to clear away the blood and sweat before flipping Crane the middle finger. Satisfaction is its own reward when the gesture wipes the cocky grin off his tanned face.

Gratification lasts seconds. Exhaustion gets the better of me, and my legs buckle. I land in a heaving heap. My head slams against the mat. I'm less than a foot from Felix's corpse. His eyes are glossed over as they stare at me in frozen serenity.

I flip on my back. The movement takes almost more effort than I have left in me. I blink against the glow of the lights as visions of my life flood my mind. Of nights raising hell with

Jester—who was known as Luke before he became Unholy. We're more brothers than friends and spent too many drunken weekends at Sanctum, the Unholy's clubhouse. We stood shoulder to shoulder the day we joined the gang and bled together more times than I can count whenever trouble came knocking on Mayhem's door.

The Unholy may not share DNA, but we're a family, and I know they're tearing the world apart looking for me.

Loyalty. Devotion. That's the only language the Unholy speak. Fuck with one of us, fuck with all of us. Ambush, abduct, and torture one of us… Yeah, you're asking for a special kind of revenge. And when I get out of here, I'm coming back with an army of Unholy to burn this fucking place to the ground.

And I *am* going home.

Question is, which version of me will return to Mayhem— the man I was before Crane took me, or the monster Gomorrah created?

Dread strangles me because of what's coming next. Crane uses liquid pain to keep us compliant. Grudgingly, I admit it's diabolically brilliant.

Medical advances were the one good to come out of America's Second Civil War. Nz822, street name noz, the one everyone calls a miracle drug, lessened a soldier's downtime after an injury. Got them healed and returned to battle within days. They even found it worked on certain types of cancers if the tumor was caught early enough. The government controls it, and that's why there's still cancer. No money in the cure. But Crane knows the right people, and noz flows like water in Gomorrah. He drowns us in it after a fight or torture session. Makes sure we're good and healed so he can hurt us all over again in an endless cycle of pain.

Fun times, man.

Ketaphrin, better known as ket, is liquid agony. It fucks with the brain's receptors, sending out empty pain signals. Labeled a crime against humanity, ket was banned after the war. But Crane has a supply chain for that, too, and uses the shit as an added layer of security. As long as he keeps us pumped with it, we're useless sacks of meat unable to defend ourselves against the sadistic guards.

When the door of the cage flies open, I snap out of my stupor, and my body tenses on instinct. Two handlers storm in brandishing cattle prods. Too battered and exhausted to resist, I lift my arms and offer them my wrists. Compliance doesn't spare me. Instead of binding me with zip ties, Lyle zaps me. I clench my teeth as electricity seizes my muscles and vibrates my bones. The stink of charred flesh sickens me—and gives me two more burns to add to the growing collection.

I struggle not to vomit as the crowd's roar of approval shakes the Coliseum. I remind myself to breathe and work to stay awake. I know what Crane does to unconscious men for the mob's amusement.

It's not pretty.

Lyle kneels beside me, syringe in hand. "Lookie what I got."

I bite back a hiss at the jab of the needle into the side of my neck. Liquid heat slides through my vein, easing the cattle prod's sting. Relief lasts seconds. In its wake comes a flood of knives that rip me apart from the inside out. As always, my dick hardens, pleasure and pain twisting in my mind until I don't know what my body loves more—agony or bliss.

Goddamn ket. When you're on it, the drug makes you need the exquisite torture on a cellular level.

See? Diabolical.

Lyle slaps my head. "You ain't sleeping, are you?"

I fight the urge to kill the prick as I push to my feet. Lyle's not done having his fun with me. A solid kick to the back of my knee nearly puts me back on my ass. I take his measure through the filthy ropes of hair hanging over my eyes. Purely on instinct, I move to lunge at him, but Thomas stops me.

His hand clamps on my shoulder. "It's not worth it."

Bullshit.

Even fucked up, I'm stronger than both guards. I can take their weapons easy and beat them half to death before anyone can charge in and stop me. But I don't, because Thomas is right, damn him. The consequences I'll face aren't worth the momentary satisfaction of breaking Lyle's jaw.

Or outright killing the asshole. At least not yet.

"He's a dead man," I growl.

"But not tonight." Thomas, who's only a few years older than me, holds out a zip tie. "Hands, Atticus."

"Not my name." I shove my arms behind me and give him my back.

"It is in here." He binds my wrists and ushers me out of the cage.

Thomas takes the lead, sandwiching me between him and Lyle. Nothing good happens when the little asshole is behind me. My muscles tense at the buzz of the cattle prod a fraction of a second before the contact tips fry me. *Again.* I trip down the three steps of the raised platform as electricity sizzles every cell in my body. My head cracks against a post. Knocked nearly unconscious, I need a second to catch my breath and for my brain to stop vibrating inside my skull.

Laughter resonates around me, but I couldn't care less. I'm beyond humiliation. Nor can I heft myself to my feet. I stay right where I am, my gaze locked on the woman in the white dress. She's too damn pretty for this place, and I can't help thinking I've seen her before. Her face is a faded dream teasing the edges of my confused mind. God, I can stare at her all night. Her flawless face fascinates me. But Lyle tugs at me, and I grit my teeth as I heft myself up.

Crane motions to his bodyguard. The buff henchman takes the lead, and Crane rises from his chair with an air of supremacy. He strolls up the aisle without a backward glance. The woman shoots to her feet and follows him, and she's so small she has to race to catch up with him. A second bodyguard completes their four-person procession as the mob parts to let them pass.

The arena snaps into focus, and I hear Thomas demand, "Seriously?"

Lyle shrugs. "Next time, he'll think twice before eyeballing me."

Thomas rubs his temples in frustration, something he often does around Lyle. The younger guard is a brat who sulks when he's chastised or doesn't get his way. "Hit him again with it, and I'm writing up a formal complaint."

As if that'll do a good goddamn thing.

"I ain't making no promises." Lyle shoves me to get me moving. "Walk, asshole."

I struggle to catch my breath as Lyle pushes me toward the back of the arena. Thomas files in behind me as we cut a slow path through the chaotic horde. My bare feet crunch down on cigar and cigarette butts, spit, spilled drinks, and God knows what else. People don't part for us as they did for Crane. Instead, they close in. Grope me. Pull at my hair. A woman launches herself at me in a blur of too much makeup and not enough clothing. She wraps herself around me, drenching my face with sloppy kisses.

I try to pry her off, but she grips me tighter. Her nails, sharpened to friggin' claws, scratch across my shoulder blades, digging trenches in the skin.

It takes Thomas and Lyle to drag her away.

"No touching," Thomas yells over the noise as he sets her on her feet.

Then we're moving again, with Lyle yanking me along.

"You gotta walk faster," Thomas urges from behind.

The fuck?

Does he think I'm moseying for the fun of it? My legs can barely support my weight.

By the time we finally make it through the crush, a guard, dressed head to foot in black tactical gear and wielding an AK-47, opens the steel door at our approach. Beyond the threshold is a corridor leading down to the dungeon. The air in here is thinner, cooler, the noise of the arena muffled. When the door closes, the click of the lock sliding into place is a harsh reality check of the insurmountable obstacles between me and freedom. Impossible hurdles I'd need to navigate to escape this waking nightmare.

Harsh fluorescent bulbs hum overhead as we trek the decline that ends in the building's bowels. Cameras, affixed to the low ceiling, are eyes in the sky watching us as we near the dungeon. The distant slap of leather against flesh mingles with a symphony of cries that grow louder the closer we get to our destination. I can't block out those wails.

Mine, I know, will join the chorus in due time.

I spent my first twenty-four years believing I was invincible.

This place cured me of my delusion real quick.

My arrogance was astounding. I thought Crane couldn't break me. Hell, I even scorned the prisoners who whimpered into the dark long after the dungeon quieted for the night. Naively thought those men were pussies. But Crane and his men are artists when it comes to pain, and our bodies are their canvases.

At the gate, Lyle blows a kiss at the camera. The door slides open, the groan and grind of metal echoing throughout the interwoven corridors.

Once we're past the first barrier, the door bangs closed behind us, sealing us inside the Hub. Two guards man the control booth, protected behind shatterproof glass. One jailer backs away from the window. Does he think I'm stupid enough to try to bust my way in, and what...? Kill them with my hands zip tied behind me? I mean, shit, I'm good, but not *that* good.

"Look who's still with us." Adam's voice sounds from a

speaker fastened above the glass. The ballsy bastard gives me a thumbs-up.

"Yep. Atticus done won himself another fight." Lyle claps me on the back over the spot where the woman scratched me. "What's this make, five wins?"

Eight.

"Congratu-fucking-lations. You get extra chow tomorrow," Pete announces.

Outstanding. Two helpings of slop. Can't wait.

"Come on." Thomas grabs me by the upper arm and hauls my half-crippled ass across the large, open area.

"Easy," I hiss.

"Geez, we're just congratulating the man," Adam grouches.

The ket's kicking in hard. The air is hot and stale, and despite the oppressive heat, I shiver as I stumble over my feet. Agony slices at my nerves with a surgeon's precision. I double over, gagging.

Lyle yanks me upright and continues through the dungeon's main chamber. "Ain't got all day."

I straighten and shuffle through the Hub, which branches off into four sections. Three corridors are blocked by steel doors. Lightweights and welterweights are kept together down one unit. Middleweights and heavyweights are housed in another. After I defeated the previous champion, they moved me from there to Elite, and I'm still deciding if the only single-celled unit's solitude is a blessing or a curse.

A gym and a disgusting, sad excuse for a shower is located down the fourth corridor. And at the very end of that hallway is the torture room. It's nasty as fuck in there, with every instrument imaginable to inflict massive damage to a human body.

Can't count how many times I've been inside that room, but it's too damn many.

Thomas unlocks the steel door and pushes it open.

Lyle shoves past him and pats his knees while making kissing sounds. "Come on, puppy. Time to get in your cage."

I'm a lot of things, but dumb isn't one of them. However, I'm hovering dangerously close to losing my shit and doing something stupid.

I shuffle over to Lyle. Get up close and personal with the fucker. "One day, you and I are gonna have a go."

By now, I have Lyle figured out. Wasn't hard. The guy is one-dimensional. He's an insecure moron who hides his short-comings behind false bravado. He wouldn't last a night in Mayhem.

Lyle's Adam's apple bobs when he swallows. "You threatening me, Atticus?"

My cruel grin is an intimidation tactic, and it works. I can smell the fear on him. "Stating a fact."

Thomas fires his cattle prod but doesn't fry me. "Back off."

Like I give a shit about being shocked again. But the ket takes full effect, and I fight against gravity as pain tries to take me down.

"Dammit," Thomas mutters. "Help me get him in the cell."

Lyle snorts. "I ain't his caretaker."

"Whatever," Thomas snaps. "Go away, Lyle."

Lyle throws a mini tantrum as he huffs out of Elite.

"You can't keep doing this." Thomas cuts the zip ties and holds out his hand.

I slap it away. "I can walk." I limp into the cell. "Lyle's a jerkoff."

"A jerkoff who can make your life miserable."

I grunt out a humorless laugh. "You're kidding, right?"

"I didn't mean…" Thomas lets the sentence trail off. "Can you get on the bed yourself, or do you need help?"

"I got it," I slur.

No, I don't, but I'll be damned if I accept a guard's help—

even if it's coming from Thomas, who's not an asshole like the others.

It takes my remaining energy to climb on the disgusting mattress. The thing is stiff, crusty, and bloodstained. It stinks of urine, and when I settle on my back and fling one arm over my eyes, I fist the other at my side, praying for sleep to come quick.

"What do you need before I go?"

Thomas and I have a strange relationship. Not friends, but not enemies. I'm still killing him along with everyone else in Gomorrah, but until then, he's the closest thing I have to an ally.

"A gun."

"Sleep it off, Atticus."

The cell door slams shut, and his footsteps fade. Lucky prick. He's walking toward freedom and fresh air.

I lie awake and stare into the darkness as I ride waves of agony and reminisce about life's simple luxuries. Hot showers. Warm food. A clean body. A soft bed. And as I finally, blissfully, float off into the abyss, I dream about an angel in a white dress.

START READING!

https://reneerocco.com/wraith

9 798218 127947